LOVE IN

INSPIRATION

D0060466

A Country Christmas

LISA CARTER

A small-town
Christmas wedding
brings surprise
blessings...

LOVE INSPIRED
INSPIRATIONAL ROMANCE

Uplifting stories of faith, forgiveness and hope.

Fall in love with stories where faith helps guide you through life's challenges, and discover the promise of a new beginning.

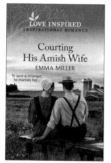

Six new books available every month!

ISBN-13: 978-1-335-59700-7

9 781335 597007

50675

EAN

LIIFC2022

"You and I need to get a few things straight, City Girl.

"First off, you can lose the bad attitude."

Kelsey bristled. "I do not have—"

"Second, we don't like each other and we never will. I get that."

For a split second, something akin to disappointment pricked her heart.

"We're from two different worlds. And never the two should meet, except they did when Nana Dot and your grandfather fell in love." His shoulders hunched. "But we both love our grandparents and want the best for them. Right?"

She sighed. "Right."

"We're never likely to be friends, but I propose we put aside our differences for their sake."

Again, there was that flicker of something. Regret? In different circumstances, she suspected Clay McKendry would have made a great friend.

She nodded, slowly. "A truce?"

"A cessation of hostilities for the duration. We need to give them wedding memories they can cherish." He jutted his jaw. "But tell me now if this is something you can get on board with."

She stuck out her hand. "We have a deal."

Lisa Carter and her family make their home in North Carolina. In addition to her Love Inspired novels, she writes romantic suspense. When she isn't writing, Lisa enjoys traveling to romantic locales, teaching writing workshops and researching her next exotic adventure. She has strong opinions on barbecue and ACC basketball. She loves to hear from readers. Connect with Lisa at lisacarterauthor.com.

Books by Lisa Carter

Love Inspired

K-9 Companions

Visit the Author Profile page at LoveInspired.com for more titles.

A Country
Christmas

Lisa Carter

LOVE INSPIRED
INSPIRATIONAL ROMANCE

LOVE INSPIRED®

INSPIRATIONAL ROMANCE

ISBN-13: 978-1-335-59700-7

A Country Christmas

For questions and comments about the quality of this book, please contact us at CustomerService@Harlequin.com.

Love Inspired
22 Adelaide St. West, 41st Floor
Toronto, Ontario M5H 4E3, Canada
www.LoveInspired.com

Printed in U.S.A.

Know therefore that the Lord thy God, he is God, the faithful God, which keepeth covenant and mercy with them that love him and keep his commandments to a thousand generations.

—*Deuteronomy* 7:9

For those who went above and beyond to stand in the gap for me as a child, thank you.

Chapter One

Families were complicated. She was running late. In a nutshell, the story of her life.

Buffeted by a brisk November wind, Kelsey Summerfield hurried down the sidewalk. Outside the Mason Jar Café, she reached for the door. A man's calloused fingertips brushed against her hand. Sparks electrified her nerve endings.

"I'm sor—" Her lip curled. "Oh, it's you."

Clay's hazel eyes narrowed. "Oh, it's you."

Last week, she'd driven over from Asheville to meet her widowed grandfather's new friend, cattle-ranch matriarch Dorothy McKendry. She'd also met Dorothy's grandson, Clay. She and the cowboy had taken a mutual dislike to each other.

She tucked a strand of hair behind her ear. "Grampy is expecting me for lunch."

Kelsey liked tall men, but not overly tall men. From her five foot four perspective, at six two Clay McKendry was definitely overly tall.

"I'm meeting Nana Dot for lunch." He reached for the door again. As did she.

Their hands touched, setting off another round of electricity. Like a scalded cat, she snatched her hand away. "I can open my own doors, thank you very much," she hissed.

She rubbed her still-tingling palm down the side of her charcoal trousers. The static electricity in the air must be off the charts today. He bowed up, crossing his arms over a massively impressive chest. Not that she was impressed. She disliked barrel-chested men.

"Opening a door for a woman is about being a gentleman." He smirked. "Your constitutional rights are in no danger from me, I assure you."

"Let me assure you—"

"While this exchange between you two has been highly entertaining and *extremely* informative—" an angular, faintly terrifying woman with ice-blue eyes and a short iron-gray cap of hair, GeorgeAnne Allen's thin lips flattened "—you're blocking the entrance to the café. The Double Name Club is waiting for me."

Did Clay's tanned, chiseled features pale a trifle?

The seventysomething ladies of the Double Name Club—more notoriously known as the Truelove Matchmakers—took the town motto Truelove, North Carolina: Where True Love Awaits a little too seriously. Her father had sent her to Truelove to prevent Grampy from falling into their clutches.

Married, divorced or spinster, *Miss* was a title of respect bestowed on any elder Southern lady. No-nonsense GeorgeAnne was the bossy one—although when it came to the Double Name Club, that was splitting hairs.

Clay yanked open the door and made a sweeping motion. "Allow me, Miss GeorgeAnne."

Lips pursed in what for GeorgeAnne passed as a smile, the uncontested leader of the matchmaker pack marched into the diner. She headed straight for the Double Name Club's favorite table under the community bulletin board.

Her compatriots in matchmaking mischief—ErmaJean Hicks, IdaLee Moore, Martha Alice Breckenridge and CoraFaye Dolan—waved her over.

Kelsey took a whiff of the tantalizing aromas of coffee, fresh-baked pastry and apple galette. Southern comfort food meets Parisian bistro. She couldn't imagine how a hick town in the Blue Ridge Mountains had managed to score such an upscale foodie establishment. Of course, it was Truelove's only eating establishment. Not exactly what she was used to in Asheville. But then, what was?

Her dad promised if she kept an eye on Grampy, he had a position for her in the family corporation. She merely had to prove herself.

Clay squeezed into the jam-packed entryway. "That was a close one."

From his beige Carhartt jacket, she caught subtle tones of leather, clean-smelling soap and a latent hint of aftershave. Her heart sped up a notch. Immediately, she squashed the vaguely happy feeling. She didn't do pleasant with Clay.

He shuddered. "GeorgeAnne called us *you two.*"

Kelsey batted her eyes. "Isn't that an Irish rock band?"

He pinched the bridge of his nose. "This isn't funny, Keltz."

A warm sensation like melted butter passed through her with lightning speed. So fast she wasn't sure she hadn't dreamed it. Her family didn't do nicknames.

She arched an eyebrow. "I'm not afraid of a bunch of old ladies sticking their powdered noses where they don't belong."

"You ought to be afraid. Very afraid," he growled in her ear.

Smelling of sweet cinnamon, his breath blew a tendril of hair against her earlobe. Another not *un*pleasant sensation. Heat crept up the collar of her sweater.

"No one plays chicken with a matchmaker and emerges unscathed. Ask my friend Sam Gibson what happened to him several Christmases ago, if you don't believe me." Removing his Stetson, Clay held the hat over his heart. "Those women have made it their personal mission to help everyone find their happily-ever-after. Whether we want them to or not."

"This town needs a collective backbone." She flicked her hair over her shoulder. "Maybe it takes someone like me to tell them to mind their own business."

"I just saved us from a long, embarrassing and possibly matrimonial entanglement."

She edged around him. "Get over yourself, McKendry."

Owner and chef Kara MacKenzie handed her a menu. "Your grandparents are waiting for you."

"They're together." He grimaced. "In the booth next to the matchmakers."

"Might as well embrace the inevitable." She elbowed him in the ribs. "There could be a Christmas wedding in your future."

He rubbed his side. "I'm not interested in settling down. I'm enjoying the field."

"This is Truelove." She made an expansive gesture. "What field?"

Waggling her fingers at him, a brunette swung around on one of the red vinyl stools lining the counter. "How ya been, Clay?" A well-dressed, cool blonde, almost as tall as him, strode past them on her way to the exit. "Hey, Clay."

"You were saying something about a field?" He shot Kelsey a look. "I'm may be the last unattached man standing in Truelove."

What she wouldn't give to wipe the self-satisfied smile off his stupid, cowboy face.

Some women loved cowboys. There was no accounting for taste. Most women probably found him ruggedly handsome and winsomely appealing.

He had the whole square-jaw, straight-nose, firm-lipped, strong-white-even-teeth thing going for him. He didn't look bad in jeans, either. But she wasn't most women. And she wasn't remotely, in this lifetime, on this planet interested in him.

"Last man standing, huh?" She followed him to the booth. "There's probably a reason for that. And not the one you imagine."

Dorothy McKendry smiled at them. "Hi, kids." Behind the wire-framed glasses, her hazel eyes had the same gold flecks as her grandson.

"Glad you could join us." Silver hair glinting under the fluorescent lighting, her grandfather motioned across the table. "Leave Clay the outside spot, honeybun. He'll need room for his long legs."

"Yeah, Keltz." He broadened his chest. "My *long* legs take up a lot of room."

She threw herself onto the bench. "Your over-size ego takes up a lot of room."

Clay sat down. "As a matter of fact, I—"

"Will you two stop fussing?" Dorothy laid her hand atop her grandson's. "We have big news."

Grampy put his arm around Dorothy's shoulders. "We're getting married."

Kelsey stared at her grandfather. This couldn't be happening. Her father would not be pleased. Not pleased at all.

Clay felt about as stunned as Kelsey looked. "What do you mean you're getting married?"

A beginning-to-be irritated expression flitted across Nana Dot's wrinkled features. "I feel sure *getting married* is fairly self-explanatory."

Beside him, Kelsey continued to open and close her mouth like a guppy drowning on air.

He fell onto the seat. "You only met in April."

Nana squeezed Howard's hand. "When you know, you know."

Kelsey's grandfather grinned. "We fell in love."

Nana Dot nodded. "The chemistry was just there."

Howard winked. "Lots of endorphins popping."

Making a choking sound, Kelsey got a deer-in-the-headlights look.

Clay leaned forward. "But at your age—"

Kelsey kicked him under the table.

Scowling, he rubbed his leg. "What I mean is, Mr. Howard, you're eighty-seven. And Nana Dot is eighty."

Mr. Howard kissed his grandmother's hand. "My child bride."

Hand to her chest, Kelsey started that hyperventilating thing again.

Nana Dot wagged her finger. "We're old enough to know what we're doing. After my dear friend, IdaLee, found happiness with her long-lost beau, Charles, we were inspired."

Clay threw a glance at the matchmaker table, uncharacteristically quiet. He should have known this outlandish notion had been matchmaker-engineered.

Howard's gaze clouded. "Kelsey, what're you thinking?"

"I think…" her mouth trembled "this is a little sudden."

Thank you, Keltz. Way to come through.

Howard lifted his chin. "At our age, we understand how short life is, and how truly precious it is to find someone special to share it with."

Clay found it difficult to swallow around the sudden boulder in his throat.

"Joan and I were married for fifty-nine years. Dorothy and her husband were married for thirty-five. We know what real love feels like." Howard opened his hands. "We want to enjoy the rest of the years God gives us as fully as possible."

Nana turned to Clay. "Last weekend at Apple Valley Orchard, Howard dropped to one knee and proposed."

"An artificial knee, mind you." Howard's eyes—the same cornflower blue as Kelsey's—twinkled. A lifetime of smile lines fanned out from the corners. "Both knees are metal, but they worked just fine, didn't they, Polka Dot?"

Kelsey gave them a slow nod. "Why can't y'all remain friends?"

Nana patted Kelsey's hand. "We considered that."

Howard shared a smile with his bride-to-be. "But we decided the platonic thing wasn't going to work for us."

Cheeks as scarlet as her winter coat, Kelsey sputtered. Clay wanted to clamp his hands over his ears. But it was too late to unhear that.

Kelsey pulled herself together. "When were you thinking of getting married, Grampy? In the spring?"

"The first weekend in December."

His jaw dropped. "That's less than a month away."

Nana scooted out of the bench. "Exactly." Howard edged out behind her.

Clay unfolded from the booth.

Kelsey scrambled out, too. "What about lunch?"

"Stay and enjoy lunch on us." With a serene smile, Nana Dot touched his cheek. "If you'll excuse us, we have wedding details to work through."

"Including putting in a call to our children." Howard stuck out his hand to Clay. "I appreciate you not making us feel like a bunch of senile, old geezers."

Clay shook his hand.

Kelsey's eyes appeared suspiciously bright. "If there's anything I can do to help, please don't hesitate to ask."

He jammed his hands in his jean pockets. "Me, too, Nana."

"I want a small wedding." A calculating look flickered across his grandmother's face. "But I might take you up on that offer." With a quick wave, the elderly couple bid them farewell.

He dropped onto the bench vacated by the geriatric sweethearts. "I didn't see that coming."

She climbed into the bench across from him. "Me, either."

"You didn't sit on my hat, did you?"

She picked his hat off the seat and handed it to him. Groaning, she buried her face in her hands. "My dad is going to kill me."

"What are we going to do about them?"

"There's not much we can do. Except for the major damage control I'll have to do with Dad." She gazed at him through her fingers and a curtain of hair. "Not a phone call I'm looking forward to taking." She smoothed the hair out of her face.

If he ran his hand through the dark brown waves of her hair, would it feel as silky against his fingertips as it looked?

Had he lost what was left of his mind? He'd met black bears more friendly than Kelsey Summerfield. He must still be in shock over Nana Dot.

The majority of the Double Name Club filed out of the restaurant seconds after the lovebirds. Not born yesterday, he figured the timing of their exit wasn't a coincidence. The double-named cronies were probably already strategizing how to further ruin his life. After the heartache with his former fiancée, they'd left him alone. Until now.

This close to Christmas, he didn't relish being caught in their matchmaking cross hairs. The holiday only prompted them to bring out the big guns of matrimonial mayhem. *Thanks, but no thanks, Double Name Club.*

And if they were considering pairing him and Mr. Howard's snobby granddaughter? The idea was beyond ridiculous. He disliked short women. Also, she wore haughty like a second skin. Then there was her face:…

Okay, so maybe he didn't dislike her face. She wasn't exactly hard on the eyes. But that mouth of hers… He inhaled sharply. Best not to go there, either.

Her blue-eyed gaze swung to him. "What?"

"Nothing."

His Aunt Trudy, a fiftysomething, hip-swinging peroxide blonde who'd worked at the Jar as long as he could remember, approached them. "Y'all gonna place an order or carp at each other all day?"

Kelsey slumped. "I've lost my appetite."

"I'll take the French special thingy I can't pronounce, a glass of water and a slice of apple galette, Aunt Trudy."

Removing a pen from behind her ear, his aunt wrote down his order. "Anything for you, Miss Summerfield?"

"Water, please." She fiddled with the sugar packets in the dispenser. "Maybe Clay will let me have a taste of his pie."

He folded his arms. "Get your own."

Aunt Trudy rapped him over the head with the order pad.

He rubbed the top of his head. "What was that for?"

"Get used to sharing, Clay." Trudy threw him an amused glance. "By Christmas, you two will be kissing kin."

What was with this *you two* business? But the image she conjured in his mind—of Kelsey's lips—lingered long after Aunt Trudy headed to the kitchen.

He got a sinking feeling that, like it or not, this Christmas was going to be one he'd never forget.

* * *

Under duress, Clay shared the apple galette with Kelsey. After lunch, they parted. She stuck around the Jar for a mocha latte caffeine kick start. She'd just stepped onto the sidewalk outside the diner when a silver GMC pickup barreled up Main Street.

With a screech of brakes, Clay pulled to a stop next to the curb. The passenger window scrolled down. "Get in."

She planted her hands on her hips. "I wouldn't get in a hurry with you, McKendry, much less a vehicle."

Leaning across the cab, he flung open the door. "Nana's taken your grandfather to the hospital."

Kelsey gasped. "What's wrong with him?"

"She didn't give specifics." His face, which usually only did scowling when he looked at her, softened. "I told Nana we'd meet them at the hospital."

This couldn't be happening. Not again. When she'd lost her mother, her emotionally distant father had abandoned her for work. A year ago, Granna had died. What would she do if she lost Grampy?

She scrambled into the truck. *Dear God, please let him be okay.*

"What happened?" She fumbled for the seat belt, but her hand shook so badly she couldn't lock it in place. "I-I can't…"

"Take a breath, Keltz."

Leaning over, Clay pulled the strap taut. Worried as he was about Nana and Mr. Howard, he couldn't help appreciating the fruity notes of perfume wafting off her. She looked delicious, and she smelled even better.

But this wasn't the time nor the place to be noticing such things about a person he didn't like. With a click, he secured her seat belt. Putting the truck in gear, he steered down Main. The pickup rattled over the bridge.

"This isn't the way to Asheville."

He blew past the Welcome sign and headed toward the corkscrew road that wound over the mountain ridge. "The closest emergency room is at the county seat."

"But they don't have the same state-of-the-art equipment as the hospital in Asheville." She jabbed her finger at him. "What kind of stupid town doesn't have an urgent care?"

He clenched his jaw tight. "The kind of town that will do anything for one of its own."

Kelsey Summerfield was exactly like his erstwhile fiancée. Last year, Angela had dumped him for the bright lights of the state capital. The litany of Angela's frequent complaints against Truelove echoed in his head. He loved Truelove, the mountains and the ranch. He never wanted to live anywhere else.

She sighed. "I do carp at you. I'm sorry."

His eyes cut to her. Maybe she wasn't exactly like his former fiancée. Angela only received apologies, never gave them.

"I appreciate you taking me to Grampy."

Angela hadn't done gratitude, either. Perhaps Kelsey wasn't the spoiled, overprivileged rich girl he believed her to be.

"When Granna passed…" Not meeting his gaze, she fiddled with the hem of her ivory sweater. "If I was to lose Grampy, too…" She stared out the window at the evergreen hillsides of spruce and fir.

An altogether new feeling stirred inside his chest. How much of her in-your-face bravado was a defense mechanism? Not unlike the pains he'd taken since the Angela debacle to steer clear of women and keep emotional attachments at a minimum.

He swallowed. "I'm sorry, too."

"I have trust issues." Her lovely lips—which again, he had no reason to be noticing—quivered. "I can be a bit of a control freak."

"No way." He threw a grin at her. "Not you."

"Amazing," she said with a laugh, "but true."

She had a nice laugh.

After Angela's betrayal, he'd self-isolated at the ranch to lick his wounds. His life became a never-ending cycle of cows, Nana Dot and occasional outings with a few buddies from high school. In truth, he was often lonely for something he didn't know how to define.

He pulled into the parking lot outside the emergency department. "Hang on a sec." He came around the hood to the passenger side. He yanked open the door and offered her his hand. "It's a jump for a vertically challenged person like yourself."

She tilted her head. "You just called me *short*, didn't you?" Her hand was soft and warm in his. "But thank you."

In the chilly winter air, their breath fogged. She let go of his hand. He immediately missed the touch of her fingers.

At the entrance, the glass doors slid open. He removed his hat. They approached the lady at the reception desk.

"We're looking for our grandparents." He could practically feel the worry radiating off Kelsey. "Dorothy McKendry and—"

Kelsey leaned over the desk as the woman typed in the name. "And Howard Summerfield."

The lady scanned the monitor. "Howard Summerfield was taken into triage about thirty minutes ago. He's being assessed by an ER physician. I'll notify the duty nurse to let Mrs. McKendry know you're waiting here in Reception. Once your grandfather is stabilized, the doctor will give you an update."

Finding a quiet corner, they sat down. Kelsey's phone rang. She declined the call.

He balanced his hat on his knee. "Do you need to get that?"

"It's my father." Her eyebrows bunched. "No need to alarm him until I find out what's happened to Grampy."

His eyes cut to her, and his heart ticked up a notch. What was it about Kelsey Summerfield that got under his skin?

To keep her from agonizing over her grandfather, he decided to keep her talking. "Favorite pizza topping?"

"Pineapple." Her mouth curved. "And you?"

"Canadian bacon."

She sighed. "Did you know my Granna died in her sleep?"

His gaze flitted to her.

She laced her hands together in her lap. "Granna hadn't been sick. We went to bed, and the next morning she was gone." She bit her lip. "I've tried to be there for him since Granna died. But he won't need me now."

Clay frowned. "Mr. Howard will always want you in his life."

"It won't be like before, though."

"Change is hard." He drew in a deep breath. "But they seem to make each other happy."

She gave him a wobbly smile. "All that matters to me is my grandfather's happiness."

Perhaps he and Kelsey weren't as different as he'd supposed.

"I'm not real good with words, Keltz." He rubbed the back of his neck. "But what a sweet gift from God. As one love story ends, another one begins."

Something inscrutable flickered in her vivid blue eyes.

The triage doors swung open. Accompanied by a sixtyish woman in a white lab coat, his grandmother emerged. Hat in hand, he rushed forward to embrace his grandmother. "What's going on, Nana?"

"We'd run to the jewelers to pick out wedding rings. Coming out of the shop, Howard dropped his keys, and that's when it happened." His grandmother introduced them to the attending physician.

"Is it a stroke?" Kelsey asked in a near whisper. "Or a heart attack?"

Tucked against his side, he could feel her shaking like a beech tree in a winter gale.

Dr. Redmayne adjusted the stethoscope hanging around her neck. "When he bent to retrieve his car keys, something tweaked in his lower back. I've given him a relaxant for the muscle spasms."

"Grampy has thrown out his back?"

The doctor nodded.

Her shoulders lowered. "That's happened before."

"Painful, but not life-threatening." The doctor tucked her hands in her coat pockets. "He'll be off his feet for two or three weeks, but I'm sending him home with a prescription to reduce the inflammation."

"The doctor says he'll need regularly applied ice-pack treatments." Nana folded her arms across her cardigan. "I'm taking Howard to the ranch so I can provide him with round-the-clock care."

An orderly wheeled Howard out to them.

Kelsey dashed forward. "Grampy!"

"Hello, honeybun."

She wrapped her arms around him.

He winced. "Gently, if you please. The old man's had a bit of an afternoon."

Dr. Redmayne touched his shoulder. "As long as he follows doctor's orders, he'll return to his normal activities within no time." The doctor reminded him to schedule a follow-up appointment and excused herself. An orderly wheeled him out to the sidewalk.

Mr. Howard winked at Clay's grandmother. "Got to be in tip-top shape for a honeymoon cruise with my new bride."

Kelsey wagged her finger. "All the more reason why I need to get you to Asheville where you can receive the best possible care."

"I'm going with Dot." Her grandfather lifted his chin. "However, Dorothy and I have a great favor to ask you, Kelsey." He took hold of Nana Dot's hand. "I want Dorothy to have the wedding of her dreams, but my injury places us further behind the wedding eight ball. Would you consider putting this wedding together for us?"

Kelsey's mouth rounded. "I'd be honored, but I've never planned a wedding before."

"You're so good with details, honeybun. Spare no expense. Put the charges on my credit card."

Clay stiffened. "I've got money put aside."

Nana shook her head. "It's taken years to save the money to increase the herd."

He widened his stance. "McKendrys pay for their own weddings."

Nana Dot pursed her lips. "I won't let you jeopardize your future by refusing Howard's generous offer."

He folded his arms across his coat. "A wedding is the responsibility of the bride's family."

"The clock is ticking, Clayton. We're on a deadline here." Nana threw Howard an affectionate glance. "We want to make that cruise."

He clenched his jaw and said no more. But this conversation wasn't over by a long shot.

"A Christmas wedding." Making *Ls* with her thumbs,

Kelsey held her hands midair, framing her vision. "The glitz. The glam. I'm thinking possibly neon uplighting."

He scowled. "Nana said she wanted a small wedding."

"Orchids." Kelsey gave her grandfather a huge smile. "Remember the Schively wedding? The acrobats in the plastic bubble? How fabulous would it be if we recreated that, but in a giant snow globe." She clapped her hands together.

Seriously?

Howard beamed at his granddaughter. "Keep those big ideas coming, honeybun."

Clay scrubbed his face with his hand. "Nana?"

His grandmother's eyes darted from Howard to Kelsey. "Truelove's church will soon be decked out for Advent. Poinsettias are Christmasy."

Mr. Howard threw his bride-to-be an apologetic look. "I'm sure Kelsey can come up with something grander that befits our special day."

Kelsey clasped her hands under her chin. "I promise you a wedding no one will ever forget."

No way was he turning Kelsey and her over-the-top ideas loose on his nana's wedding day.

He thrust out his chin. "I'll help Kelsey plan the wedding."

Nana's shoulders visibly relaxed. "That would be such a relief to have you on board, dear heart."

Howard's forehead creased.

Nana touched her fingers to her mouth. "I mean, there's so much work to be done in such a short time." She tilted her head at her groom. "How wonderful it would be for both our grandchildren to work on this project together."

Clay leaned against the wall. "We'll be co-planners."

Kelsey frowned. "You have a cattle ranch to run."

He broadened his shoulders. "Winter is our slower time."

"While this is so incredibly generous of you, Clay..." She moistened her bottom lip. "And sweet of you to offer..." The crinkle in her nose belied the sincerity of her words. "Your assistance is completely unnecessary." She gave him a bright, totally fake smile. "I'd hate to waste your valuable time."

"I don't consider giving my nana and your grandfather their special day a waste of my time."

Spots of red peppered her cheeks. "I don't need your help."

"Actually, you do." He glared back. "And you're going to have my help whether you want it or not." He threw her a lopsided smile. "For the next few weeks, consider us joined at the hip."

"You are impossible," she growled.

"Thank you." He smirked. "I try."

He vowed to do everything in his power to prevent Kelsey Summerfield from turning Nana Dot's wedding into a circus.

Chapter Two

Clay retrieved Howard's car from the parking deck for Nana Dot to drive back to Truelove.

Grampy was obviously in a great deal of physical discomfort. With some maneuvering, Clay helped him lie flat in the back seat. In the truck, Kelsey and Clay followed behind Nana Dot over the winding mountain road toward the McKendry ranch.

She laced her hands together. "About you being a co-planner for the wedding."

He gripped the steering wheel. "Now is not the best time to hash this out."

Veering off the secondary road, he steered the truck through the crossbars of the Bar None Ranch. Split-rail fencing lined the long, graveled drive. Trees edged the perimeter of the pastureland.

Her first impression of the McKendry home was that it was exactly that—a home. A wraparound porch encircled the two-story, white Queen Anne Victorian.

She took a deep breath of the clean, crisp mountain air. The ranch house reminded her of the homes along Asheville's Montford Avenue in the historic district. Like something out of an American fairy tale, the house sat on a knoll with three-hundred-and-sixty-degree views of the rolling Blue Ridge horizon.

He parked beside her grandfather's sedan. She caught a glimpse of a picturesque red barn, a corral, and other outbuildings. In a distant field, cattle grazed.

Miss Dot headed to the kitchen to prepare an ice pack. With Kelsey on one side and Clay on the other, they helped her grandfather shuffle along to the guest bedroom. They eased him onto the mattress. But she still believed his camping out at the McKendry's was a mistake. Stubborn was a well-known Summerfield trait. She could do stubborn, too.

"What about your clothes and toiletries, Grampy?"

"I made a few calls. The condo manager is going to let Dorothy's neighbor, Jack Dolan, inside my place to pack a few of my things and bring them to the ranch."

"But I could've—"

Clay's grandmother bustled in with an ice pack in her hand. She fussed about for a few moments, situating the pack, fluffing a pillow, drawing a blanket. Kelsey stepped out of her way.

"No need to bother, Kelsey." Grampy threw Dorothy a brilliant smile. "My bride will take good care of me, won't you, sweetheart?"

She fingered the strap of her purse. "It wouldn't be a bother, Grampy."

The condo at the ski resort was west of Truelove, nearer to Tennessee. Decades ago, he'd been one of the first commercial real-estate developers to see the potential for skiing in the North Carolina mountains. Unable to bear the memories of the Asheville home he'd shared with Granna, last spring Grampy had fled there to the family's vacation home.

"It's nearly dusk." He glanced out the window overlook-

ing the ridge of mountains. "You should start for home."
He closed his eyes.

Clay's grandmother became brisk. "Howard needs to rest."

Feeling dismissed, she bit her lip against the treacherous sting of tears. Might as well get used to it. From now on, this was obviously how it was going to be. Subdued, she followed Clay to his truck.

She'd left her car parked outside the Mason Jar. Lunch seemed a lifetime ago. A tense silence reigned between her and Clay on the way down the mountain into town.

Keeping to her side of the pickup, she darted a quick glance at his clamped jaw. He drummed his fingers on the wheel. Her gaze returned to the scenery flashing by the window.

The glorious autumn splendor, for which the Blue Ridge was famous, had passed. The trees stood bare, the branches stark against a gunmetal sky. Brown leaves littered the roadside. Only the evergreen firs and cedars dotting the landscape relieved the bleakness of the cold November afternoon. Winter was upon them. She shivered.

Brows constricting, he reached for the dial on the instrument console. "I can turn up the heat."

"No, thank you. I'm fine."

Once the sun descended behind the ridge, darkness fell swiftly this time of year. She wasn't used to driving the steep mountain roads outside the city.

His forehead creased. "Will you be all right returning to Asheville tonight?"

She had the ridiculous urge to smooth the line away. Someone ought to tell him scowling would ruin his cowboy good looks. But not her. She didn't like cowboys.

"You could stay over at the ranch," he added.

"No." She flinched. That had come out harsher than she intended. "I should get back to my apartment. I'll be fine."

"So you keep saying." A muscle jumped in that well-chiseled jaw of his. "Sorry the ranch isn't the five-star accommodation you're used to."

Kelsey scowled at him. "That wasn't what I meant." But he was determined to cast her as a rich-girl snob. Seeing Grampy with Miss Dot was hard. Tired and more than a little blue, she wasn't up to returning to the ranch.

"As a young woman, Nana Dot trained as a nurse." He strangled the wheel. "Your grandfather will be in good hands."

She gave him a nice view of her back. They passed the Welcome to Truelove sign. "*Where true love awaits*," she muttered to the windowpane.

The truck rattled over the bridge into town. The river swirled below. As tumultuous as her fragmented emotions.

"Seems to have worked for Nana Dot and Mr. Howard."

Kelsey sniffed. "Hasn't it just."

"That's it."

He jerked the wheel and pulled into the vacant parking lot of the bank. She threw him a startled glance.

"You and I need to get a few things straight, City Girl." He turned in the seat. "First off, you can lose the bad attitude."

Kelsey bristled. "I do not have—"

"Second, we don't like each other, and we never will. I get that."

For a split second, something akin to disappointment pricked her heart, but she rallied. "Listen, Clayton..."

He grimaced as she'd known he would. He didn't like to be called by his full name. However, it was just too fun to resist pushing his buttons.

"If you're done throwing your debutante tantrum..."

Her eyes widened. "I am not throwing—"

"Were you or were you not a debutante?"

She glowered. "That is beside the point."

He folded his arms across his chest. "It is precisely the point."

She hated herself for noticing the play of muscle under his shirt.

"We're from two different worlds. And never the two should meet, except they did when Nana Dot and your grandfather fell in love." His shoulders hunched. "But we both love our grandparents and want the best for them. Right?"

She sighed. "Right."

He dropped his arms. "We're never likely to be friends, but I propose we put aside our differences for their sakes."

Again, there was that flicker of something. Regret? In different circumstances, she suspected Clay McKendry would have made a great friend.

She nodded, slowly. "A truce?"

"A cessation of hostilities for the duration. We need to give them wedding memories they can cherish." He jutted his jaw. "But tell me now before we go any further down this road of enforced association if this is something you can get on board with or not."

He made it sound like spending time with her was a prison sentence. Good to know up front how he really felt about her. *Fine. Be that way.* Never let it be said, though, she'd done anything less than her best for Grampy's sake.

She stuck out her hand. "We have a deal."

For a second, he stared at her hand. Was he recalling the spark of electricity between them earlier? Her cheeks flamed. Her heartbeat sounded alarmingly loud.

Taking her hand, his palm felt strong, warm and calloused from hard work against her own. Disappointment rose at the loss of camaraderie they'd shared at the hospital. But it was clear how he viewed her—a frivolous creature who'd never done an honest day's work in her life. She was used to being underestimated by her father. She'd show Clay McKendry. She'd show them all.

He turned his hand over, his palm up. "Let me see your phone."

"What?"

"I'll put in my number." Avoiding her gaze, his voice went gruff. "Text me when you get to Asheville. I want to make sure you make it home safely."

She blinked at him. Just when she'd been working up a head of steam, he went all cowboy-gentleman on her.

"Over the next few weeks, we'll need to be in close contact." His features went ruddy. "I mean—"

She suspected underneath his cowboy toughness there lay a streak of sweetness he didn't like to reveal. And just like that, the atmosphere between them became less frosty.

"Close contact." She laughed. "Got it."

"We'll need to stay in touch to plan the wedding," he growled.

She handed him her cell. "Of course."

He typed in his number and gave it back to her. "What's first on your wedding to-do list?"

"I'll research area venues and, if there's any openings, pay them a visit."

He nodded. "I want to go with you to check them out."

She opened her mouth to argue but decided not to waste her breath.

Putting the truck into gear, he eased out of the parking lot and continued down Main Street. After business hours, the café was shuttered. Downtown, such as it was, was largely deserted. Everyone had gone home to enjoy the evening with their families. Her spirits sank lower. She had only cheese and crackers waiting to welcome her at the apartment. To borrow a bit of cowboy slang, *Yippee.*

He steered into an empty slot next to her blue Subaru.

"I'll let you know what I discover." She reached for the door. "At this late date, there may not be any facilities available for the weekend of the wedding."

"Where there's a will, there's a way. If there's a way, I have full faith Kelsey Summerfield will find it."

"Thanks for the endorsement." Her lips quirked. "I think." She slipped out of the truck.

"Keltz?"

At the friendly shortening of her name, an inexplicable relief flooded her senses.

"You won't forget to text me?" He leaned across the seat as far as his seat belt allowed. "I'll worry if you don't."

Something squeezed inside her rib cage. No one had bothered to worry about her since Granna died. "I won't forget." She tucked a strand of hair behind her ear. "I promise."

"Good." Frowning, he turned his face toward the closed café. "Better get on the road now."

He made no move to leave until she backed out of the space. Someone had raised him right. She'd seen no evidence of his parents at the Bar None. What was the story there? The cowboy was proving more intriguing than she'd imagined.

It was dark when she pulled into her apartment complex, but despite the events of the day she felt considerably lighter than when she'd left the ranch. She ran up the flight of stairs and let herself inside the apartment. Shrugging off her coat, she texted Clay.

A second later, a squiggling line of dots appeared. Had he been watching for her text?

Let's talk tomorrow.

Kicking off her shoes, she smiled and typed. Will do.

Good night, City Girl.

Her heart did a little zing. Good night, Cowboy. She hit Send.

The doorbell rang. Such was her buoyancy, she didn't stop to look through the peephole but flung open the door.

"Why haven't you answered my calls?" Her father glared. "You and I, young lady, need to have a long, over-due chat." Boyd Howard Summerfield III strode past her into the apartment.

Her happy feelings sank faster than the ship that hit the iceberg.

She choked off a sigh. "Dad?"

His beige wool overcoat fanned out behind him. Not one to stand on ceremony—or an invitation—he marched over to her couch and sat down. "I was in a meeting when your brother texted me your grandfather had gotten en-gaged." He perched on the edge of the cushion. "When my father couldn't reach me, he contacted Andrew and left it to him to break the news of his impending nuptials. When's the date?"

"The first weekend in December," she whispered.

Her father leaned forward with his elbows on his knees. His mouth twisted. "Why am I the last to hear this news?"

Because he couldn't be bothered to check his phone or email unless it involved business? She sank into an adja-cent armchair.

Her father's eyes—the same color she'd inherited from Grampy—became an icy blue. "I sent you to that one-stop hick town to avoid this very situation."

She bit her lip.

"You had one job." He stabbed his fingers through his

beginning-to-gray dark hair. "How is it once again you've managed to fail me?"

Since the moment of her birth, she'd never been anything but a disappointment to him. Her stomach tightened. She could kiss any prospective position in the family business goodbye.

"As for my dear old dad," her father huffed, "has he gone senile?"

Kelsey stiffened. It was one thing to castigate her many shortcomings, but it was quite another to attack Grampy. "For the first time since Granna died, he's actually happy. He's in love with Dorothy, and she loves him."

"She's a gold digger." Her father sneered. "That ranch is barely breaking even. Maybe she thinks in marrying a Summerfield, she'll put the ranch in the black for the first time in years."

Kelsey's eyes widened. "You did a background check on the McKendrys?"

He arched his eyebrow. "Did you doubt that I would? After you met this Dorothy person last week, the first thing I did was contact a private investigator."

"Grampy would be mortified if he knew what you've done."

"Don't be naïve." Her father's gaze snapped to hers. "He did the same thing when your mother and I became engaged. Where do you think I acquired my business acumen from, if not from the old barracuda himself? Nothing personal. Merely good business practice."

The man her father described in no way resembled the grandfather she'd known and loved her entire life.

"Dorothy is not a gold digger." Kelsey straightened. "The McKendrys aren't like that."

"Humans are like that, Kelsey."

When had he become so cynical? But she knew. After the slow, inch-by-inch death of her mother.

"Granna would want Grampy to be happy."

Her father stood abruptly. "My mother's barely been dead a year. Has he no respect for her memory?" Her dad paced the length of the sofa. "But what would someone your age know about loss?" He sat down again.

Kelsey knew plenty about loss. She'd lost Granna and her mom just as much as her dad had. But she could never say such a thing to him. He'd never understand.

Might as well tell him the rest, though.

Taking a breath, she told him about the pulled muscle and Grampy's insistence on staying at the ranch. "He's asked me to plan the wedding." She opened her hands. "Please don't ruin his happiness, Dad. This is the most alive I've seen him in months."

Her father's eyes narrowed. "You don't think there's any changing his mind, then?"

"I don't." She gripped the armrests. "I'm sorry."

"Don't be sorry. Fix this, Kelsey."

She frowned. "I'm not sure—"

"The Summerfields have a reputation to maintain." Her father lifted his chin. "Can I trust you to put together an event that will do us proud?"

"Of course."

His eyes bored into hers. "Pull this off, and you'll have earned a permanent position in the family company." He rose. "I'll expect regular progress reports."

This was her chance to prove herself and earn his respect. Perhaps his affection, too. Or was that too much to hope for?

Heart racing, she walked him to the door. "I promise you a spectacular wedding no one will ever forget."

Chapter Three

Clay didn't get much sleep that night. Wide awake before sunrise, he arose earlier than usual and headed out for morning chores. His breath puffed in the frosty air. It was the perfect time to make repairs and get ready for the late-winter calving season.

Under the electric lights in the barn, he spent an hour working on the tractor. Later, his stomach growling, he made his way across the barnyard to the kitchen.

Nana Dot handed him a steaming cup of coffee.

He warmed his hands around the mug. "Thanks." He nudged his chin toward the hallway. "How's the patient this morning?"

"Not an early riser." Nana handed him a plate of hotcakes. "Unless it's tee time."

He dug into the food. It wasn't many mornings he beat his grandmother out of bed. The lovebirds would have to adjust their routines to each other.

Clay placed his plate in the dishwasher.

"You're not the only early riser, though." Nana scrolled through her cell phone. "Howard's granddaughter isn't one to let any grass grow under her feet. She's texted me four times already this morning."

He glanced at the clock. "What about?"

"What else?" His grandmother heaved a sigh. "The wedding of the century."

He chuckled. "She can be a lot."

Nana threw him a contrite look. "I shouldn't complain. She's handling details I would never have thought to consider."

"But four texts? All before seven?"

"She's a go-getter." Nana raised her eyebrows. "She's definitely got the bit between her teeth. She's put together something she calls a wedding storyboard. And there's a checklist."

"Nana, if this is too much—"

"She means well. She's just very…" Nana's mouth worked "…enthusiastic."

He slipped his arms into his coat. "This is your wedding, not hers. I won't let her steamroll you."

"Last text included a questionnaire. Favorite colors. Favorite foods. Food I dislike. Colors I dislike." Nana tilted her head. "You get the picture."

He was getting the picture, all right. Kelsey Summerfield was nothing if not intense. And exhausting. "Should I have a word with her?"

Nana shook her head. "She wants Howard and I to send the names and addresses on our guest list."

"I'll be out in the barn if you need my help with Mr. Howard."

Standing on the back porch, he filled his lungs with the apple-crisp mountain air and then got to work shoveling out the pens.

He couldn't imagine his grandmother living anywhere but the ranch. Howard would soon become a permanent fixture at the Bar None. The ranch had been Clay's home his entire life, but after the wedding, where did that leave him? Sharing the farmhouse with the octogenarian new-lyweds?

Clay better get a social life of his own, or he'd find himself third-wheeling forever.

His cell vibrated. Removing his work gloves, he fished it out of his pocket. He couldn't help but smile when he saw the caller. When she wasn't completely driving him insane, Kelsey made him laugh. "What's up?"

"If you're too busy doing ranch stuff . . ."

He stuffed his gloves in his pocket. "I'm not too busy."

"What're you doing?"

He leaned on the handle of the shovel. "Cleaning cow stalls."

There was a beat of silence. "What does that involve?"

He bit back a smile. "A shovel and a wheelbarrow."

"Does this involve cow excrement?"

Always such a hoot talking to Kelsey Summerfield. "Yes, it does."

"Gross."

He pictured Kelsey crinkling her cute little nose. "What're you doing so early on this bright November morning?"

"I found several possible venues worth checking out. But since you're busy, I'll visit them."

"Nice try, Keltz, but I'm not doing anything that can't be done another time. Where are they located?"

"One is in Asheville."

He frowned. "I was hoping for something nearer True-love."

"The second is closer. Out in the country."

Resting the shovel against the gate, he propped himself against the wall. "That sounds promising."

"I think so."

Why did he get the feeling she wasn't telling him everything? "What's the game plan?"

"I have an appointment to view the one in Asheville at ten o'clock this morning and the second one around eleven thirty. Do you want to meet me at the first location?"

He swiped his forehead with his forearm. "How about I pick you up and we ride over there together?"

"Great. I'll text you my address. How soon can you be here?"

He straightened. "I need to shower, but give me an hour and a half, and I'll be there."

"With bells on."

His brow scrunched. "What?"

"Christmas wedding bells. 'tis the season, Cowboy."

He returned to the house for a quick shower. Because they were probably going to some glitzy places, he put on an almost-new pair of Wranglers he usually only wore to church. And took the time to iron a shirt.

When he came out of his room, Nana was fixing a breakfast tray for Mr. Howard. "Don't you look fresh as the first snowfall on the ridge."

Clay smiled. "Don't want uptown Asheville to think we're a bunch of hicks." He told his grandmother about the day's mission.

"Howard and I composed our guest list while you were in the barn. I've emailed it to you and Kelsey."

Clay carried the tray down the hall for her. He stuck his head inside the guest bedroom and bid Mr. Howard good morning. He handed off the tray. "Don't know when I'll be back, but I'll see you when I see you."

"Have fun. Try not to argue." Nana leaned closer for his ears only. "And don't let her get carried away."

After double-checking his GPS, he pulled into her apartment complex without any trouble. He hurried up the three flights of stairs and rang the doorbell. Trouble answered the door.

"Hi, Cowboy." Kelsey beamed at him. "I'm ready if you are."

Trouble with a capital *T*.

Gulping, he took in the early morning vision that was Kelsey Summerfield. She wore a winter-white sweater that looked like soft cashmere and skinny jeans tucked into a pair of knee-high black boots. Wow.

He jammed his hands into his pockets. "I was born ready, City Girl."

She slipped on a wool coat the same bright blue color as an April sky over the ranch and ducked her head through the strap of a cross-body soft leather purse. He did a quick scan of her apartment. Chic and stylish—just as he would've supposed in this swanky high-rent district in downtown Asheville—but the white, modern decor seemed surprisingly comfortable, too.

At the truck, she gave him the address of the first venue.

She motioned down the block toward a parked, red double-decker bus turned coffee shop. "I belong to a monthly book club that meets there. Outdoor seating only, so this time of year we relocate to nearby Woolworth's for coffee and pie." Her eyes sparkled. "What's the last book you read?"

He steered the truck toward the River Arts District. "There's not much time to read at the ranch. If I get still, I tend to fall asleep."

"Maybe you haven't come across the right story yet."

He looked at her. "Maybe I haven't." He looked away. "Tell me about the book you're reading this month."

The story revolved around a man and a woman on the run after she witnessed a drug-cartel execution. While bullets flew, romance blossomed. Kelsey had reached the climatic, all-hope-is-lost part when he turned into the parking lot of a former textile mill, closed for nearly a hundred years.

He pushed back the brim of his hat. "Is this the right place?"

"It is." She gave him a smile. "Repurposed as an event venue. My brother, Andrew, got married in a place like this about a decade ago."

He hadn't known she had a brother. "A decade ago? That would have made you either a very old flower girl or a very young bridesmaid."

She laughed. "I'll have you know I was the best junior bridesmaid there ever was."

Outside the steel-fronted entrance, he stared at the brick building. "I don't know about this."

She cocked her head. "Give it a chance."

The venue director ushered them into the large open space with vaulted ceilings and steel beams. "Did I understand from our phone conversation you are a Summerfield?" the woman purred.

He stiffened.

Kelsey's smile faltered. "I am." She inserted her hand into the crook of his arm. "This is Clay McKendry."

Country and proud of it, he broadened his shoulders.

"Historic. Industrial." In stilettos, dramatic makeup and a sleek, high-powered business suit, the platinum-blonde paused beside one of the cathedral windows overlooking the French Broad, the same river that flowed past Truelove. "Urban chic."

As the director showed them around, Kelsey fired questions at her. He peered over her shoulder at the checklist on her phone.

"Every love story is different." The director rested her perfectly manicured hand on the exposed brick wall. "And so are we."

The venue felt cold and sterile.

At the end of the tour, the woman led them to the entrance. "The beginning of your forever starts here."

"Oh. The venue is not for us." Kelsey's eyes cut to him. "We're not together. I mean, obviously we are together." Her hand waggled back and forth between the two of them. "Here. Today. But we're not together-together, as in like, getting married."

"Ain't that the truth," he muttered.

She glowered at him. "We're here on behalf of family members."

He jammed his hat on his head and pulled her toward the door. "We'll give you a call if we're interested." He hustled her out.

"What did you think about the venue?"

He lifted his hat, ran his hand over his head and clamped the Stetson back on again. "It doesn't seem like Nana's kind of place." He sighed. "I'm sorry."

"No, you're right."

He did a double take. "Come again?"

"I wasn't feeling the Nana vibe, either."

"Where to next?"

"Prepare to be amazed, Cowboy."

He had an idea every day with Kelsey would feel pretty amazing.

The property lay between Asheville and Truelove. During the drive, he had only to insert a topic into the conversation, wait for the coin to drop and let her go. He enjoyed her animation and enthusiasm for life. Her hands in constant motion, she leaped from one quirky subject to the next. Possessing wide-ranging tastes, she touted favorite emojis—

"You have a favorite emoji?" He shook himself. "Of course you'd have a favorite emoji."

Pistachios were her favorite nut.

He rolled his eyes. "Why does it not surprise me you have a favorite nut?"

She ignored him. "This will probably gross you out, but my favorite sushi restaurant is—"

"I like sushi."

"Wait." Her mouth dropped. "What?"

"And you had me pegged as a strictly meat-and-potatoes kind of guy. Although, I never refuse a good steak."

"Way to wow, Cowboy." Her eyes shone. "I had no idea behind the swagger and rakishly dimpled chin, you had such hidden depths."

An unexpected, quicksilver warmth shot through him. "I'm a deep kind of guy." He fingered his rakishly dimpled chin.

Turned out they liked the same local North Carolina band. He wouldn't have seen that coming. Kelsey Summerfield liked contemporary indie folk music.

She settled against the seat. "I've been doing most of the talking."

"Well, when you're good at something—Ow!" He rubbed his side where she'd elbowed him, but it was worth it to push her buttons.

"Can I ask you a personal question?" She bit her bottom lip, and his heart accelerated.

She snapped her fingers in his face. "Are you listening to me?"

He wrested his attention off her mouth. "Yes, ma'am."

She chewed her lip again, and his heart did a nosedive. *Stop with the lip-nibbling.* It was playing havoc with his equilibrium. *For the love of Christmas, Keltz...*

He'd missed her question. "Say it again, please."

She gave him an exasperated look. "There were lots of

photos at the ranch house, but I got the impression you and Miss Dot lived there alone. I wondered…"

"You wondered what?"

She fingered the strap of her purse. "About your parents."

He one-handed the wheel. "What about 'em?"

"They're still alive, right?"

He nodded. "Very much so, thankfully."

"But they don't live at the ranch?" She waved her hand. "Forget I asked. None of my business. If anyone understands complicated families, it's me."

From the remarks she'd made yesterday, her father sounded like a real piece of work.

"My dad grew up on the ranch and helped Nana run it after my grandfather died. The ranch was never my dad's passion."

"But ranching is yours?"

"When I finished school, I took over as operations manager, and my parents retired to the coast, where my mom was born. They visit for the holidays, and I visit them during the summer. I'm happy they're happy. They love living within sight and sound of the ocean."

"But not you?"

He shrugged. "The mountains call me, not the sea. What's your passion?"

"I'm not sure yet. Mountains surround Asheville, too. I love the combination of eclectic energy and historic ambience there." She stared at the passing scenery. "For a foodie like me, it's a culinary hot spot."

He veered onto a long, asphalt drive. "Truelove has its own small-town charms."

"If you say so." A *V* formed in the delicate space between her brows. "You were okay with taking over the ranch, right?"

"I can't imagine wanting to do anything else."

"Good." She glanced away. "There's nothing worse than having your future mapped out for you."

Was she speaking from personal experience? "What is it you do when you're not trying to be the boss of everything?"

She snorted. "I call it *utilizing leadership skills*."

"Whatever," he grunted. "Or perhaps Summerfields don't have to work for a living like the rest of us."

"My father is the most hardworking person I know. Too hardworking." She glared at him. "My brother and I were expected to earn our places in the family firm. Since Grampy retired, my dad is the president and chief executive officer. Andrew is now the chief financial officer. My sister-in-law, Nicola, serves as general counsel."

"What is your role in the family biz?"

"To be determined." She fidgeted. "I have a business degree. I organize the yearly golf tournament that the company sponsors and various publicity launches." Her mouth turned downward. "My father has high standards for his children. I'm still working on proving to him I deserve a permanent role in the corporation."

Her father's standards sounded impossible to meet. Not that it was any of his business.

The road wound around the mountain like stripes on a candy cane before emerging from the trees into a grassy meadow with an honest-to-goodness—

His eyes widened. "A castle?"

The gray stone castle, with a turreted tower and moat, overlooked the valley below. He pulled into a graveled parking lot. "What is a castle doing in western North Carolina? Is this for real?" He cut the engine.

"Surprise!" Throwing open the door, she hopped out. "Totally real. A hundred years ago, an eccentric railroad baron dismantled a medieval castle in the Scottish Highlands and rebuilt it stone by stone here in the Blue Ridge. Isn't it awesome?"

They climbed a series of terraced steps. At the top, they ambled across the open drawbridge toward the stout iron-studded oak door.

Clay scrubbed the stubble on his jaw. "It's something, all right."

Her cell dinged. She read the incoming message. "The manager is on a business call. The door is open, and he says for us to look around. He'll be with us shortly."

Clay lifted the iron latch and pushed the heavy door open with his shoulder. The hinges creaked. His eyebrows arched. "Very atmospheric."

She marched inside. "Welcome to Castle Doone."

"Doom is right," he muttered.

He eyed the shiny armor-clad, life-size medieval knight standing guard at the foot of the stairs that led to the minstrel gallery. The Great Hall was crisscrossed with gigantic oak beams from which heraldic banners hung.

"I love it." Arms outstretched, she did a slow, three-hundred-and-sixty-degree turn. "Don't you love it?"

He didn't love it.

"Seems like something out of a horror movie with a dash of romance novel thrown in for good measure."

She propped her hands on her hips. "It's romantic. Like something out of a fairy tale."

He took off his hat. "I don't mean to keep raining on your wedding-princess fantasies, but this doesn't seem like the cozy, homestyle wedding Nana is going for, either."

"When the king and queen are in love, a castle becomes a home."

He folded his arms. "You're an expert on being in love, I suppose?"

She pursed her lips. "I didn't say that."

"Have you ever been in love?"

She flushed. "I don't see how that has anything to do with—"

"Answer the question." He wasn't sure why he'd thrown down that gauntlet, but a sudden, desperate need to know burned a hole in his belly. "Have you ever been in love?"

"Not yet. What about you? Have you ever been in love?"

"Yes. No. Maybe." He scoured his face with his hand. "At least, at the time I believed I was."

"Whoever she was, she hurt you." Kelsey's voice softened. "I'm sorry."

Unable to bear the sympathy in her gaze, he faced the armor-plated knight. "No big deal."

"It must've been a big deal for you to have lost your faith in happily-ever-afters."

"Angela and I…" He shrugged, striving for a nonchalance he didn't feel. "We were too different. It would've never worked. Better we found out before it was too late."

Kelsey nodded. "If it's meant to be, it will be."

He crimped the brim of his hat. "I guess you adhere to the old adage that everything works out for the best in the end."

"Absolutely." She waved her hands. "If it isn't the ending you hoped for, then it's not the end."

He cut his eyes at her. "My philosophy is closer to *It may not be the party you hoped for, but while you're there you might as well dance.*"

"You're referring to the *playing the field* thing you mentioned yesterday?"

"Why not?" He threw her a crooked grin, which usually drove the females wild but on her appeared to have little effect.

She cocked her head. "How exactly is that working out for you, Clayton, other than in the obvious short term?"

His grin faded.

"Grampy and Miss Dot inspire me. At their age, finding love again." She sighed. "Here's hoping I won't have to wait till I'm in my eighties to be swept off my feet by love, though."

He couldn't imagine why some city dude hadn't swept her off her feet already. The men in Asheville must be a dim bunch.

"Before you completely nix the idea, let me show you what I put together on the storyboard for this place." She rummaged through the voluminous leather purse and took out a large sketch pad. "Imagine if we used this end of the Hall for the ceremony. Think swags of evergreen on the beams. Dozens of candles." She thrust the pad at him.

Kelsey strode toward the other end of the Great Hall. "We could set up high-backed chairs with the bride and groom at the head of a horseshoe-shaped table, presiding over a sumptuous medieval feast."

Sketchbook in hand, he joined her.

Kelsey seized his arm. "And madrigals. Oh, Clay." Her voice rose in concert with her imagination. "Imagine madrigal singers crooning Christmas carols."

"Only word I understood was *horseshoe*."

"Think of the possibilities. Bagpipes. Who doesn't love a bagpipe?"

Clay could think of several people.

Her hands created an imaginary viewfinder again. "I'm seeing a blue-and-green tartan."

Clay folded his arms against his chest. "I'm not wearing a kilt, Kelsey. Absolutely not. Get it out of your head. Not happening."

"Have you no cultural pride?" She threw open her hands. "For the love of haggis, you're a McKendry."

"I do not love haggis, and I'm a McKendry from the

highlands of North Carolina, not the Highlands of Scotland." He scowled. "I'm not wearing a dress."

She clung to his arm. "It's not a dress."

"You can stop batting those big blue eyes at me, Keltz."

She fluttered her lashes. "You'd absolutely rock a kilt, Clay. You'd be even more irresistibly handsome."

Kelsey believed him handsome?

Nonetheless, he hardened his resolve. "I'm not wearing a kilt. Not for you. Not for Nana. Not for love nor money."

"Fine. Be that way, Mr. Fun Killer." Letting go of his arm, she gave him a small push. "Clay McKendry, where dreams go to die."

He laughed. She laughed, too. A burly man with a long white beard emerged from the nether regions of the castle keep.

After a few logistical questions, she shook her head. "I'm afraid the site won't work for our wedding party."

Given her previous enthusiasm, Clay stared at her perplexed.

"Have you checked out the guest list?"

Clay shook his head.

"Between the bride and groom and older friends like the matchmakers, while absolutely dreamy, the castle won't work for them." She motioned. "Too many stairs from the parking lot. Not accessible."

She thanked the manager for his time, and they exited.

"I would've never thought about that." He took hold of her elbow as they negotiated their way down the stone steps to the truck. "You are good at this. Your granddad was right to put you in charge of this shindig."

"Thank you." She sagged against the truck. "But this means we're down to only one option."

"You were thinking to secure a venue today?"

"What choice do I have? We're already playing catch-up. Everything else was booked months ago. I can't fail Grampy or my dad again."

He looked at her sharply. "What's this got to do with your father?"

"Dad wants to be kept in the loop about Grampy's nuptials." She gave him a wobbly smile. "I texted him this morning about the castle and the mill. If this last option doesn't work out…"

He reached for her hand, surprising himself as much as her. "What happened to *if it's not the ending you hoped for, it's not the end*?"

"I hate that you are using my own words against me," she growled.

"We're only thirty minutes from Truelove. Let's have lunch at the Jar and refuel." He squeezed her hand. "Everything will look brighter after we put some grub in our bellies."

"I feel certain Kara would object to calling her gourmet cuisine *grub*, but I take your point." She laced her fingers in his. "I didn't think I needed a co-planner, but turns out I do. Thanks for not leaving me to muddle through this alone." Her voice hitched. "And for being a friend."

At the catch in her voice, his heart did a funny sort of twang. Opening the truck door, she climbed inside. Yet as he made his way around to slip behind the wheel, it wasn't food he had on his mind.

But rather a happy/not-happy feeling—that Kelsey Summerfield saw him as her friend.

Chapter Four

"For such a small person, you sure put away the food." Clay cocked his head. He signaled his Aunt Trudy for the bill.

Looming professional or personal disaster tended to have that effect on Kelsey. After this latest failure, Dad would never give her another chance to show what she could do.

Sidling over, Trudy laid the bill on the table. Kelsey reached for it, but he intercepted it first.

"I pay my own way, Clayton."

His eyes narrowed. "I've got this."

Trudy's gaze ping-ponged between them. Behind the cutout window to the kitchen, a bell dinged. "You know the drill. Pay at the register when you're done wrangling." She moved to pick up another order.

"Whatever floats your horse, Ginger." Kelsey fluttered her hand. "Next time's on me."

He gritted his teeth. "I'm not a ginger."

She snorted. "There's none so blind than those who refuse to look into a mirror, Gingersnaps."

"I have brown hair." He ran a hand over his head. "With red-ish highlights."

"To-may-to. To-mah-to." She shrugged. "Still red."

"You are impossible."

She smirked. "I try."

His mouth twitched. "You succeed." He glanced around the always-crowded diner. "Listen, I just got a text from Allen's Hardware. A part I ordered has come in. Since we're in town, would you mind if I went over there to get it before we head to the next venue?"

She put down her coffee mug. "No problem."

"Why don't you sit tight here and finish your latte?" He grabbed hold of the edge of the table. "Won't take me but a few minutes. I'll be right back." Clapping his hat on his head, he hauled himself out of the booth.

After paying, he exited the diner. Peering through the picture window overlooking the town square, her eyes followed the broad set of his shoulders until he crossed Main and disappeared around the corner.

She lifted her gaze to the distant horizon. Wave upon wave of undulating blue-green ridges enfolded the charming town like the worn but comforting arms of a beloved grandmother. The mountains defined the citizens of Truelove. As did the gushing river that wound around the town like a horseshoe.

"Mind if I join you for a minute?"

Jolting, she put a hand to her throat.

"I didn't mean to startle you."

The seventysomething woman's bright blue eyes twinkled behind the wire-framed glasses. Eons ago, she and Kelsey's grandmother, Joan, had been roommates at nearby Ashmont College.

Kelsey gestured toward the seat Clay had vacated.

Martha Alice Breckenridge threw her a small smile. "Quite the view, isn't it?"

Hoping she referred to the oak trees lining the perimeter of the village green, Kelsey lifted her chin. "Truelove is a lovely little town."

The elegant, older woman touched her perfectly coiffed silver white hair. "Our cowboys aren't too bad, either."

Kelsey went crimson.

Martha Alice patted her hand. "I'm teasing." Then she spoiled the effect by chuckling a tad wickedly.

"I have an appointment at Hair Raisers soon, but I've found a photo album from my school days with your grandmother you might like to see." Granna's lifelong best friend gave her the gentlest of smiles. "I miss her, too. Everyday."

Kelsey's mouth trembled. "I'd love to see the pictures sometime, Miss Marth'Alice."

She abbreviated the matchmaker's name the same way Granna had.

"I'm happy for Dorothy and Howard." Martha Alice reached across the table and took Kelsey's hand. "I think Joan would be, too."

Tears pricked her eyes. Martha Alice wasn't wrong. That was exactly what Granna would have wanted for the man who'd been the love of her life.

Martha Alice squeezed her hand. "Howard's been adrift since Joan left us. Once you've had time to grapple through your naturally mixed emotions, I think you'll find, as I have over the years, that our greatest joy lies in seeing the happiness of those we love most."

"I'm trying, Miss Marth'Alice."

Martha Alice made a vague motion in the general direction of the vacant Double Name Club's favorite table. "I also hear you've taken on the planning of the nuptials."

"A month's notice isn't much time, but I'm giving it everything I've got." She gave Granna's friend a quick rundown on the morning's disappointing results.

"What you've got is plenty." Martha Alice nodded. "But

the long commute to oversee the details is going to eat up valuable time and energy. What would you think about staying with me until the wedding?"

Truelove offered neither a hotel, bed-and-breakfast or any other rentable accommodations. "I couldn't impose on you like that, Miss Marth'Alice."

"You'd be doing me a favor." Martha Alice waved a wrinkled, blue-veined hand. "Since my granddaughter Kate married her own cowboy and moved to Jack's ranch this summer, the house feels much too empty for me to rattle around in alone, especially as we approach the holidays. What do you say?"

"I'd love to take you up on your offer." She took a breath. Already the wedding felt less overwhelming and more doable. "Thank you."

Martha Alice nudged her chin at the window. "I think your cowboy is on his way to claim you."

"Clay is not my cowboy."

"Whatever you say, sweetie. I must be off." Martha Alice inched out of the booth. "I didn't see your car out front."

"Clayton picked me up this morning at my apartment." She used her best prim schoolmarm voice, but the effect seemed wasted on Martha Alice, who laughed.

"Perfect. You can retrieve your things and drive your car back to Truelove. I'll see you tomorrow at home."

Since Granna died, home had become an elusive concept for Kelsey. She flicked a glance at the tall, muscular figure of the cowboy making his way down the sidewalk. Something pinged in her heart. He really was quite heart-stopping to look at. She got out of the booth. Too bad he was so annoying and a cowboy to boot.

Kelsey and Martha Alice walked out to the sidewalk.

The older woman gave her a hug. "If there's anything I can do to help with the planning, please don't hesitate to ask. Dorothy has a lot of friends in Truelove who'd love to chip in. That's one of the things I love most about this town. Everyone truly looks after their neighbors."

If she was referring to the Double Name Club... Kelsey pursed her lips. Their so-called help she could do without.

Clay walked up to them. She and Martha Alice said goodbye. The older woman strolled toward her car, only to stop for a chat with her garden buddy and fellow matchmaker, ErmaJean Hicks.

He offered his arm. "Ready for our next adventure?"

She could practically feel ErmaJean eyeballing them.

Kelsey whacked his bicep. "Have you lost what little mind you possess?"

Forehead creasing, he rubbed his arm. "What was that for?"

"They are everywhere." She looked left then right. "Watching. Plotting. Conniving."

He craned his head in both directions. "Who?"

She smacked his arm again. "Can you be any more obvious?" she hissed.

He chuckled. "Does this involve the Irish rock band?"

"Very funny." She grimaced. "I'm talking about giving a totally wrong impression. The *you two* thingy."

"A matchmaker behind every bush?" Crossing his arms across his coat, he rocked onto his heels. "Good to know I've made a believer out of you. Give 'em an inch and they'll take a matrimonial mile."

"Cowboy and City Girl?" She made an exaggerated shudder. "It doesn't bear contemplating."

"My feelings exactly. Marriage—a fate worse than death."

Did he mean marriage in general or more specifically marriage to her? She experienced a surge of extreme dislike for a woman she'd never met. That Angela person had done a real number on his heart and his head. Ruining him for anyone else. Including her?

She sucked in a quick breath. Where had that come from?

Opening the truck door, he offered his hand. When he smiled at her, it was all she could do not to swoon. Clay McKendry was the whole package. A gentleman and easy on the eyes, too.

The more time she spent with the cowboy, the less outlandish the idea of a relationship beyond friendship appeared.

We're just friends. But to her chagrin, the possibility of something more had taken root in her heart. Suddenly, friendship with Clay had lost some of its charm.

The third venue option, a wedding destination resort, was on the other side of Truelove. At a higher elevation, a dusting of snow covered the ground. She told him about her upcoming relocation to Martha Alice's house.

Clay rapped his thumb against the steering wheel. "Favorite joke?"

"I have the perfect joke for November." She perked. "April showers bring May flowers. What do May flowers bring?"

He shrugged. "I don't know. What?"

"Pilgrims."

He groaned.

"Get it? *Mayflower*?" She nudged him. "Pilgrims?"

"I got it." He rolled his eyes. "Sounds like a kid joke."

She grinned. "I get my best jokes from my five-year-old niece, Eloise."

"I didn't know you had a niece."

She glanced at the passing scenery. "Andrew and Nicola are super busy, and I don't get to see her nearly as much as I'd like. But we have our special traditions, just the two of us."

"Like what?"

"Every February fourteenth, we have a standing sleepover at my apartment while Andrew and Nicola go to dinner. We call it Galentine's."

He chuckled.

"Grampy told me your sister has kids."

"My nephew, Peter, is also five. My niece is three going on forty-three." He flicked his eyes at her. "She has the same *leadership* skills as you."

"I like her already."

At the sign for the resort, he turned off the main road. "How did you hear about this place?"

"One of my suite mates in college was married here a few years ago. You might know her. She grew up in True-love, but her family moved to Asheville after she graduated high school."

"Her father an attorney?"

She smiled. "He specializes in real estate. He and my dad do a lot of business together."

He cut a glance at Kelsey. "Her wedding was quite the shindig."

She turned in the seat. "I don't remember seeing you. Were you there, too?"

He shook his head. "My friend, Sam, attended. He told me about it."

"Sam… I remember him. He's very handsome, isn't he?"

Clay stiffened. "If you like the blond, blue-eyed jock type, I guess."

"No need to get a bur up your saddle. Merely making an observation. To each his own." She fluttered her lashes at him. "Some women prefer gingers."

"I am not a—" *Wait. Did some women include her?*

The truck crested the hill. Below them, the majestic,

white-columned historic inn nestled in the sweep of a snow-covered valley.

Her eyes shone. "It's like something out of a winter wonderland, isn't it?"

The resort's clientele weren't exactly the sort of people the McKendrys rubbed shoulders with, but the place was spectacular. His stomach tanked. No way could he afford to put on a wedding here. Something of his feelings must have shown on his face or—scary thought—Kelsey knew him better than he supposed.

Releasing her seat belt, she slid across the seat and laced her fingers through his. "My father's company sponsors a golf tournament here every spring. The resort's bottom line owes us big time. I promise there'll be a deep discount."

"It would have to be a huge discount, and even then…" It meant a lot to him she respected his need to pay for Nana's wedding.

She squeezed his hand. "I can be very persuasive."

For inexplicable reasons, his gaze drifted to her mouth. "Don't I know it," he rasped. His heart sped up. She tilted her face to him. He leaned forward. Her lips parted.

His insides somersaulted. What was happening here? This would not do. Not do at all.

Clay thrust open the door. "We should get going," he grunted.

Jumping out of the cab, he hurried around to the passenger side. She gave him a curious look, but she didn't comment on what almost happened in the truck.

What *had* almost happened in the truck? Nothing, thanks to his quick sense of self-preservation. Had he so quickly forgotten the painful lessons he'd learned courtesy of Angela? *Fool me once…*

They followed the sidewalk to the imposing front entrance. He darted glances at her, but Kelsey kept her fea-

tures averted. Was she upset with him? For a host of
reasons, he and the city girl were not a good idea. Good
thing he'd pulled the plug. But if so, why was his stomach
in a knot all of a sudden?

Inside the lobby, an ornate chandelier glittered above
their heads. He yanked his hat off his head and clutched
it over the place his heart used to reside before Angela.

Expensive oriental carpets lay scattered around the
white marble floor. Clustered on the formal, silk-covered
chairs and sofas, guests conversed in low voices.

The sinking feeling deepened. "Why did I let you talk
me into coming here?" This was going to be humiliating.

But he suspected there were few people on earth who
could withstand the human dynamo known as Kelsey
Summerfield when she got the bull by the horns.

"If the price was affordable, can you see Miss Dot liking it enough to get married here?"

"Who wouldn't like it?" He raked his hand over his
head. "My grandmother has worked her fingers to the bone
her entire life. It's not a matter of whether she would like it
or not—she deserves pampering. But no way can I spring
for this, Keltz." He felt his cheeks burn. "The McKendrys
are not in the same financial league as the Summerfields,
and I won't let your family foot the bill."

"Will you trust me to negotiate the best price?" She
looked at him. "A price within your means?"

He pinched the bridge between his brows. "How do you
know what I can afford?"

She didn't say anything.

"Nana?" He growled. "She told you what's in my herd
fund, didn't she?"

"Trust me." She twined her hand in his. "I've got this.
And you."

She tugged him toward the registration desk.

A middle-aged woman in a navy-blue suit keyed in their names. "You have an appointment with our events director, I see." She picked up a phone. "I'll let Mr. Randleman know you've arrived."

Kelsey adjusted the strap of her purse on her shoulder. "Thank you."

A scarecrow of a man in an expensive coat and tie soon joined them.

Beaming like the events coordinator was her nearest and dearest long-lost friend, Kelsey introduced him to Clay. Mr. Randleman led them across a richly carpeted hallway to his office. He gestured for them to take a seat in a pair of dark leather chairs and then settled himself behind a massive mahogany desk.

She gave Mr. Randleman the lowdown on the wedding they were putting together for their grandparents. Then she went into business mode. "Over the years, my father has brought a lot of money into the resort's coffers."

Looking down his long, sharp nose, Randleman gave her an oily smile. "It's been a profitable and rewarding partnership on both sides of the table."

"All true." She placed her hands on the armrests. "I'm looking for the resort to offer me a substantial incentive to host my dear grandfather's wedding here." Her gaze bored into his. She didn't blink.

Mr. Randleman shifted his weight. The chair squeaked. "Less than four weeks to put together an occasion of this nature is rather last-minute, Miss Summerfield."

Uncrossing her legs, she planted her feet firmly on the carpet. "Your administrative assistant assured me the date was open. I trust you've had time to peruse the details I emailed this morning.

"I have."

She arched her eyebrow. "I feel sure your impeccable

staff can handle the small, intimate wedding we're proposing. Give me a figure, Mr. Randleman."

Clay had never glimpsed this side of her before—serious, driven. He was impressed. More than impressed.

Reaching for a piece of ivory stationery embossed with the resort's logo, Randleman scribbled a number. He slid it over the desk to her.

Clay swallowed past the boulder clogging his throat. Sweat broke out on his brow.

She scanned it and shoved it back. "Try again." She threw him a smile as sharp as a barracuda's teeth. "Unless you're no longer interested in doing business with the Summerfields."

"There's no need to be hasty." Randleman held up both palms. "I'm sure we can work something out to our mutual satisfaction." He jotted down another number and handed it to her.

Her features betrayed neither elation nor disapproval. "I assume this figure is all-inclusive. The rehearsal dinner? Catering for the wedding reception, including place settings and linens?"

Randleman removed a monogrammed white handkerchief from his coat pocket and mopped his forehead. "If that is what you wish…"

"It is." She leaned forward. "I think the terms will suit us fine. I'd like to sign the contract before we leave the premises."

"Of course."

Giving the man a dazzling smile, she rose. Not sure what had just happened, Clay rose as well.

She extended her hand across the desk. "As always, such a pleasure doing business with you, Mr. Randleman. My father will be pleased."

Randleman shook her hand. "I'll have my assistant prepare the documents."

"While we wait, I'd like to take Mr. McKendry around the property to show him my vision for the wedding weekend."

Randleman ushered them out. "I'll make sure the paperwork is ready when you return."

What astronomical sum had she committed him to? Clay hardly noticed where she led him. They'd exited the main building and ventured onto a cobblestone terrace behind the inn.

"We'll hold the rehearsal dinner here." She let go of his arm. "Imagine twinkle lights strung around the perimeter." She gestured to the enormous stone fireplace. "A roaring fire. Linen-clad round tables. Gas heaters to keep the guests warm under the blue-velvet sky glittering with stars."

He had to give it to her. Kelsey Summerfield could probably sell ice to polar bears.

This would bankrupt the Bar None.

"Wouldn't it be fabulous if there was snow the weekend of the wedding like now?" She pulled him down the stone steps toward a paved path that curved around a bend of trees. "Let's pray for that."

It was getting late in the day. Once the sun disappeared behind the ridge, darkness fell fast. Already the lavender shadows cast by the inn lengthened across the snow-covered vale.

He followed her along the path through a snow-daubed glade of evergreens lit by strings of fairy lights. The tangy scent of pine permeated the air. The small, stone chapel lay around the bend. Lights glowed through the stained-glass windows, spilling colorful reflections on the snow.

"Isn't it lovely?" She clasped her hands underneath her chin. "So romantic."

His gaze darted to her. "Very lovely." He wasn't thinking of the chapel.

But the setting *was* very picturesque. And in present company, extremely romantic.

A smile curving her lips, she tucked a dark tendril of hair behind her ear. His heart did that funny rat-a-tat-tat thing it did when he thought about her hair. And when she looked at him like she was looking at him right now with those shining big blue eyes of hers...

He could always take out a second mortgage on the ranch. Sell his truck.

"Don't you want to ask how much you're in for this wedding?"

Actually, no, but he supposed he had to face reality sometime. He squeezed his eyes shut. "Let me have it."

She named a figure.

His eyes shot open. "That can't be right, Keltz."

"I assure you it is."

Was she telling him the real price?

He made a grab for her hand. "Let me see that paper." His breath fogged in the chilly air.

She handed it to him with a flourish. "I told you to let me handle Randleman."

The number she'd quoted had been entirely accurate. He wouldn't have to mortgage the ranch. Or sell his truck. The cost would deplete his herd fund but give it a year—or two—and he'd be able to replenish it.

"It's called the art of negotiation."

"You were impressive." He toed the ground with his boot. "But I don't like to take advantage—"

"Advantage?" She hooted. "Shall I tell you how much commission Randleman makes every year off the golf tournament alone, not to mention the quarterly corporate weekends we throw his way?"

The sum she named made him weak in the knees. So much money. Her seeming lack of regard for it made his head swim. In terms of social aspirations, Angela had been a wannabe, but Kelsey was the real deal.

Which drove home their utter incompatibility in regard to social standing. And like a dose of ice water in the face, eradicating any ideas of anything between them beyond friendship.

She took him inside the small chapel with the red carpeted aisle running between two sections of wooden pews. Later, they returned to the main inn for him to sign the contract. There were lots of other details that according to Kelsey needed ironing out, but twilight would be fast upon them. He still needed to take her back to Asheville and return to Truelove. She made an appointment to talk further with Felicity, their own personal wedding coordinator at the resort, to discuss rehearsal-dinner and reception-food options.

On the road, he strangled the wheel, consumed by the insurmountable differences between them.

She didn't notice his silence. "Now that we have a venue, I can order the invitations. I'll have to expedite the printing and send them through the mail ASAP." She kept up a running monologue about color schemes and something she called *tablescapes*.

With three weeks, four days and countless hours of enforced proximity until D-Day ahead of him, he'd have to be extra vigilant in guarding his affections when it came to the bubbly and effervescent Kelsey Summerfield.

They were polar opposites. Like night and day. Rather forcibly, he reminded himself of his post-Angela policy toward women. *Keep it light and at arm's length.*

He stole a side-look at her. Totally in her element, she gave him a happy smile. His gut clenched. Beguiling, that's what she was. Simply beguiling. His shoulders slumped.

Arm's length might prove easier said than done.

Chapter Five

Clay had acted preoccupied on the ride to Asheville, but ever the gentleman he insisted on escorting her to the door of her apartment.

Wishing to prolong their time together for reasons she preferred not to examine, Kelsey reached for her cell. "Stay for dinner. We should nail down the information for the invitations. I can order take-out sushi."

He looked over the railing toward the parking lot below. "No, thanks."

Tired of wedding planning? Or of her company?

She leaned against the door. "I could order a pizza instead."

He hunched his shoulders. "Can't stay. Sorry."

Okay... Tired of her.

He stuffed his hands in his jean pockets. "Got to get back. Early morning. Chores tomorrow."

Clay McKendry wasn't the most talkative person she'd ever known, but this evening he'd taken *stoic* and *taciturn* to a whole different level. Like he had to pay for every word he let pass between his lips. Her gaze flickered to his mouth. She flushed, recalling the split second at the resort when she'd thought for a crazy, impossible moment he meant to kiss her.

Obviously, in light of his current awkward behavior, a stress-induced hallucination on her part.

She straightened. "Right. Thanks for helping me sort out the venues today."

He took a step back. "No problem." He cut his eyes again toward his truck. Anxious to be away? "Good night."

Kelsey went inside. What was up with him? And people said women were moody?

Shaking her head, she ordered the sushi, anyway. While she waited for the delivery, she sent a quick text to her father, updating him that a venue had been secured.

Dancing dots appeared.

She curled up on the sofa, pulled a pillow cushion to her chest and laid the cell on top.

Mill or castle?

A warm feeling filled her. An unexpected blessing from Grampy's wedding. How wonderful was it that she and her dad were talking. Communicating more than they ever had before. He was finally showing an interest in one of her projects.

Neither, she typed. Much better.

A few seconds later, more squiggly dots. Where?

Before she could respond, the doorbell rang. She lay aside the phone and retrieved her order. After eating, she packed a suitcase for her stay with Martha Alice. That night, she dreamed of castles, cowboys and Christmas.

The next morning, she ran around Asheville, gathering invitation samples and meeting with a couple of prospective DJs Felicity had recommended.

She made an effort to keep Clay in the loop, texting

him about what she discovered. But his replies left a great deal to be desired. Monosyllabic words like *Fine* or *Good* finally devolved to thumbs-up emojis.

It was midafternoon before she headed to Truelove. He said he wanted to be her co-planner. He said winter was his slower time. What was his deal?

After an early dinner at Martha Alice's, she looked through the long-ago photos of Granna and her best friend at nearby Ashmont. They laughed at the bygone hairstyles and fashion choices of the postwar era.

She made a note on her cell to set up an appointment for Dorothy with the wedding boutique in Asheville. She also realized she'd neglected to answer her father's text about the venue. She picked up her phone.

"What flowers does Dorothy want in her bouquet?"

Kelsey laid aside her cell. "She told me to use my own judgment. One more thing on my to-do list."

"You're a natural at this. I am so impressed at your level of organization." Martha Alice set down her teacup. "You could do this professionally."

"Thank you. But let's hold off on the praise until after I get on the other side of the nuptials. This is my first foray into planning a wedding, but I've been a bridesmaid in a gazillion weddings." She shook her head. "Always the bridesmaid, never the bride."

"Think how prepared you'll be when your turn comes." Martha Alice's blue eyes twinkled. "Which, based on the attentiveness of a certain Truelove cowboy, may come sooner than later."

"It's not like that... We're not like that." She blushed. "Dad says the sensible thing is to establish my career before focusing on matters of the heart."

"The heart almost never does the sensible thing, though, does it?" She arched an eyebrow. "From what your grandmother Joan told me regarding your father's whirlwind courtship of your mother, he didn't exactly follow his own advice. They eloped."

She hadn't known that about her parents. It was hard to imagine her buttoned-up, unemotional father throwing caution and sensibility to the wind for love.

"I'm going for a winter-wonderland theme." Best to get Martha Alice off Kelsey's nonexistent, never-going-to-happen romance with Clay McKendry. "What flowers would you recommend?"

An avid gardener, Martha Alice mentioned a specific rose with velvety crimson petals.

Kelsey pulled up a photo on her phone. "I love it."

"Particularly stunning when paired with white roses." Martha Alice smiled over her teacup. "All-white weddings are elegant, but I do love a pop of color."

"I want to finish off Miss Dot's bouquet with a silver-edged, royal-blue velvet ribbon I found on the internet."

Martha Alice also had some fabulous ideas regarding Christmas tablescapes and wedding decor. Over the next few days, she ticked more items off her list. Felicity at the resort had proven incredibly helpful. They hit it off, and Kelsey began to consider her a friend.

She talked with her grandfather at least once a day. To her relief, he sounded stronger and in great spirits, especially when they discussed the impending wedding.

Dorothy had put him onto a set of daily stretching exercises to strengthen his back muscles. Kelsey would have loved to spend more time with him, but she wasn't entirely sure what the frequency or protocol should be for visiting the ranch.

Being with Martha Alice was like having Granna back. She suspected the older woman enjoyed their time together as much as Kelsey did. It was wonderful to have someone to bounce ideas off. Earlier in the week, she'd believed she was reaching a similar kind of comfortable rapport with Clay, but he'd gone radio-silent.

She lay awake at night worrying she'd unknowingly offended him.

Although always kind and polite, Dorothy wasn't her family. The ranch wasn't her home. They hadn't acquired the drop-in-anytime level of familiarity. Kelsey wondered if they ever would.

She did her best to keep Clay's grandmother apprised of every step in the planning process. Yet there were important details on the checklist that required the immediate and personal okay of the bride and groom. And she was more than a little peeved at Clay.

The next day, she called Dorothy to see if it was okay to stop by the ranch to finalize the couple's music selections for the reception. When she arrived at the Bar None, Clay's truck was parked outside the barn, but he was nowhere in sight.

Grampy was in a chipper mood. No longer confined to bed, he had progressed to sitting in a leather recliner in the living room. Kelsey sat down on the couch. With Dorothy in the flanking recliner, they went over the list of songs.

"These are great." Kelsey smiled. Classic, golden oldies from the most romantic era of American music. "I'll forward the list to the DJ."

"Something else you should be aware of." Dorothy stuck out her chin as if expecting an argument. "I've decided to ask the pastor of my church in Truelove to marry us."

"Reverend Bryant offered to do our premarital counseling." Grampy snorted. "I was married longer the first time than he's been alive."

"Nevertheless," Dorothy's voice held a touch of frost. "I've learned from experience that whether a couple is eighteen or eighty, there are topics that should be thoroughly discussed to eliminate later misunderstandings."

Kelsey glanced between them.

"Whatever you think best, dear." Grampy shrugged, but he didn't look as if he totally agreed.

His marriage to Granna had been idyllic, or so it had seemed to Kelsey. But maybe Dorothy's first marriage hadn't been as carefree. Not that it was any of her business.

She laid her cell on the cushion. "If you give me his contact information, I'll coordinate wedding details with him directly."

Dorothy removed a business card from a side table. She handed it across to Kelsey. On the table, Kelsey spotted a stiff, black hat brush. Like for a Stetson? An uneasy suspicion needled at her gut. Had Grampy's new favorite seat actually been Clay's seat first?

She felt a pang of sympathy for the irksome cowboy, dispossessed from his favorite chair. The familiar routine of his normal life had been as upended as her own by the sudden engagement. Larger than life, Grampy could be a bit much. And unthinkingly presumptuous. How was Clay coping? Was he okay?

Not that he'd appreciate any concern from her. His absence had made that abundantly clear.

She pulled up the to-do list on her phone. "What about the wedding party?"

Grampy shifted in his—Clay's—chair. "I'll ask your dad to be my best man."

She smiled. "I'm sure he'll be pleased." She told them about his unexpected interest in the wedding planning, leaving out the background check.

Dorothy folded her hands in her lap. "I've asked my son, Gary, Clay's father, to walk me down the aisle." Her gaze flicked to her groom. "Clay will stand up as one of Howard's groomsmen along with your brother, Andrew."

Grampy cleared his throat. "Dorothy's great-grand-daughter is too young to be a flower girl. We want to ask Eloise."

"Oh, Grampy." Kelsey pressed the cell phone to her chest. "She'll be thrilled."

"My great-grandson, Peter, is old enough to be ring bearer. I've asked my daughter, Trudy, to be my matron of honor." Dorothy frowned. "Although since she's divorced, I'm not sure if the proper designation should be *matron* or *maid*."

"Dorothy's granddaughter, Rebecca, Clay's sister, will also stand up with her." Grampy gave Kelsey a big smile. "In addition to your planning duties, I think you should be a bridesmaid, too."

Grampy's idea? Or Miss Dot's? It would have been better if Dorothy had asked Kelsey herself. But with his characteristic exuberance, maybe Grampy had simply beat his bride to the punch. The older woman's placid gaze gave nothing away.

Had Miss Dot felt pressured by Grampy into issuing the invitation?

"Thank you, Miss Dot," she murmured. "It would be an honor to be one of your bridesmaids."

Grampy nodded, clearly pleased. Miss Dot's thin lips creased into a small smile.

An eternal optimist, Kelsey put aside her doubts. The wedding had the makings of a real family celebration. Home and family—the two things she had longed for her entire life. This union would bring together two very different families into one brand-new harmonious whole.

"There's still one crucial item that needs to be taken care of right away."

Dorothy tilted her head. "What's that?"

"Shopping for the wedding dress." Wedding planning was turning out to be fun. Who knew she'd enjoy it so much? "There's a shop with an enormous selection near Asheville."

Miss Dot's eyes narrowed. "It doesn't require an enormous budget, does it?"

"They have a dress for every budget," Kelsey reassured her. "Thousands—and I mean that literally—to choose from. We're sure to find a dress you'll fall in love with."

Grampy chuckled. "Too late for that." He laid his hand atop the table between them. "She's already fallen in love with me, haven't you, Polka Dot?"

Her eyes crinkling into a smile, Dorothy placed her hand in his. "Absolutely."

"I hate to rush this, but your dress and what the bridesmaids wear is one of the more time-sensitive items, in case we need to make alterations."

Dorothy nodded. "Best make the trip before the weather turns."

"Why don't we ask Trudy to come with us?"

Dorothy's lined cheeks lifted. "Trudy would love that."

They made plans to travel to Asheville the next day. Hesitant to leave Grampy unattended for so long, Dorothy called the ranch next door to ask CoraFaye Dolan if she could drop in to make sure he got his lunch. Cora-Faye promised to keep Kelsey's grandfather company in her absence.

"I don't need a babysitter," he said, fuming.

Dorothy got off the phone. "There's nothing like Truelove when it comes to good neighbors."

Kelsey felt a pang of envy at the community camaraderie. She didn't know any of her neighbors in Asheville, and she'd lived in her apartment for three years. One of the bigger drawbacks to city life.

In Truelove, where the sidewalks rolled up at the end of the business day, night life consisted only of the stars. But throw a cowboy into that mix… Suddenly, night life in Truelove held an appeal all its own.

Flustered, she perused her checklist. "Speaking of wedding attire, Grampy already owns a perfectly suitable tuxedo. I'll get Dad and Andrew to stop by the men's formalwear shop where Grampy bought his so the tuxes will match."

Despite her determination not to ask about Clay, every few minutes she couldn't help her attention from straying out the window toward the barn.

"I'll have the shop coordinate with a sister store in Boone where Dorothy's great-grandson lives, and another store near Clay's father at the coast so they can be sized. Once the bridesmaid dresses are chosen, the bridal boutique will do the same for your granddaughter, Miss Dot."

Her eyes drifted toward the window again.

This time, Dorothy caught her. "Perhaps Clay should accompany us tomorrow so he can get measured for his tux."

A telltale flush heated her cheeks.

"I'm not sure where my grandson has taken himself." Dorothy smiled. "Clay usually comes in for a hot cup of coffee about this time every afternoon. Would you do me a favor, Kelsey?"

She sat forward on the edge of the leather sofa. "Sure."

Dorothy rose. "Would you take a thermos out to Clay for me? He must be extremely busy not to have come inside for his usual break."

Or hoping to avoid Kelsey. Unable to think of a good excuse to refuse his grandmother's request, she found herself, thermos in hand, tromping across the barnyard in search of the elusive cowboy.

He wasn't in the barn. She followed the thunk of an ax to an area behind one of the sheds. The slanted rays of the sun glinted off the coppery tints in his supposed brown hair. He'd shed his coat and hat, which hung from a nearby fence post. In shirtsleeves rolled to his elbows, he raised the ax over his head. He brought it down with a loud smack onto an upright piece of wood, cleaving the log in half.

Maybe sensing someone had come up behind him, his shoulder blades tensed.

"It's me," she rasped. "Kelsey."

Gripping the ax casually in one hand, he turned.

Unsure of her welcome, she bit off the smile that rose on her lips.

He frowned. "I didn't expect to see you. Here. Today."

Cringing at the idea he might think her one of those silly Truelove women who chased after him, she thrust the thermos at him. Somehow without realizing it, either she'd taken several paces toward him or he'd moved closer to her. But regardless, the thermos made hard contact with the equally hard muscles in his abdomen.

He grunted.

"Sorry." About to beat a hasty retreat, his free hand closed over hers, pinning her and the thermos in place.

"What's this?"

His gravelly voice triggered swirling loop-de-loops in her belly. Her breathing suddenly sounded extraordinarily loud to her own ears. "Coffee. Miss Dot. You."

She threw him her most charming smile, hoping to draw him out. A smile she'd learned at Granna's knee. Honed to perfection during a long-ago debutante season. A smile she put on for her father's business associates.

However, the rugged, chiseled planes of his face didn't

alter. She got nothing from him. Zilch. Nada. No more teasing. No more giving as good as he got.

Yanking her hand free, she took an enormous backstep. "Don't want to hold you up from your…your…." she gestured at the ax "…lumberjack thingy."

Just before she spun on her heel, she thought she saw his lips twitch. "Bye." She waggled her fingers over her shoulder.

A wall had gone up between them, and she wasn't sure why.

"No, wait." She whirled around to face him. "I also wanted to say I'm sorry."

He blinked. "Excuse me?"

She opened her hands. "I know I can be too much. That's why Dad sent me to live with Grampy in the first place after Mom died." She was babbling. Something she did when she was nervous. "Whatever I said or did that offended you, I'm sorry."

He dropped the ax on the ground at his feet. "Your father did what?"

She clapped her hand over her mouth. She hadn't meant to let that part slip out. She'd never actually said that aloud to another human being in her life. Not even Granna. Mortified, she did an about-face.

"Keltz—"

She'd made an absolute fool of herself. Wishing the earth would swallow her whole, she dashed toward her car.

His longer legs ate up the distance between them. "Wait. Please." At the corner of the barn, he caught hold of her coat.

"You have nothing to be sorry about. Kelsey. Would you look at me?"

Her eyes darted from her boots to his face.

"I apologize for leaving you to deal with the wedding by yourself. I should've been there for you."

"You're busy with the ranch." She fretted the ends of her fringed scarf. "I can handle the wedding planning."

Somehow he'd known even before she'd called out or he turned around, she was near. It was like he had a sort of extrasensory awareness when it came to her. "I'm not that busy."

Kelsey motioned at the ax, lying in the dirt. "The lumberjack thing…"

"I was cutting cedar fence stays."

"Do the fences at the Bar None have a tendency to wander, Clay?"

He told himself not to laugh. "Fence stays reinforce a fence between the posts." He leaned one shoulder against the shed wall. "So the fence wire doesn't sag or gap." She smelled good, but then she always smelled good to him. Something flowery that sent his pulse pounding.

"I've worn panty hose that did that." Her expression remained deadpan. "So annoying."

He laughed outright. For the love of Christmas, he'd missed her. He'd missed her wacky humor and this thing— whatever it was, the thing he was afraid to give a name to—that resonated between them.

"I'll have to take your word for it in regards to hosiery." He raked his hand through his hair. "But it's also annoying in ranching when the cattle escape through the gaps, and I have to round them up again."

She looked at him with those beautiful, expressive eyes of hers. "I thought maybe if…" she bit her lip, and he believed his knees might buckle "…if wedding planning doesn't interest you—"

"I adore wedding planning."

She cut him a look. "Or if having to keep company with me isn't to your liking—"

"Keeping company with you is the best part of wedding planning."

Her mouth curved, but the smile quickly faded. "Then, I don't understand the silent treatment."

Clay's heart clenched. His self-imposed isolation had hurt her feelings. The last thing on earth he ever wanted to do. He blew out a breath. "It isn't you. This is my issue."

"Is there anything I can do to help?"

He shook his head. "Just something I need to work through on my own." The arm's-length strategy wasn't turning out like he'd planned. If anything, it had only made him think about her more, while denying himself the pleasure of her company.

Clay shuffled his boots. "What did you mean about your father?"

"It's not important."

She would have fled again if he'd not snagged her arm. "If it's important to you, it's important to me."

She leveled a stare at him that made him squirm. "Why?"

Fence wire wasn't the only thing that needed mending today.

He scoured his face with his hand. "Because I care about you. Because we're friends."

"Is that what we are, Clay?"

Her gaze locked onto his. His heart jackhammered. He had to remind himself to breathe. When she gazed at him like that, he had a hard time recalling his own name, much less thinking.

"Keltz," he whispered.

Unable to resist the impulse, he wound his index finger around a tendril of dark hair that dangled against her neck. Her hair was soft and silky, just as he'd supposed.

A Country Christmas

Something gentled in her face. She gave him a genuine smile. Not like the flirtatious, armor-plated, hostess-with-the-mostest smile she turned on at will for people like Randleman at the resort.

"After my mother died, my father was unable to tolerate my presence for long stretches of time. He chose to bury himself in the firm. I lived with Granna and Grampy until I graduated."

Something that felt like an actual physical pain lanced his heart. He'd treated her exactly like that cold-hearted excuse for a father of hers. A man Clay in no way wished to resemble.

"I didn't know that about your relationship with your father."

She laughed. The sound was utterly devoid of mirth. "We don't really have a relationship." She sighed. "Hence my overzealous enthusiasm to impress him with Grampy's wedding."

He couldn't begin to imagine what Kelsey could have done—what any child of Clay's could ever do—to cause Clay to turn his back on them. How old had she been when her father had exiled her from his home and affections? Clay had lots of questions, but now was not the time to probe further.

"Thank you for trusting me with that." Did Nana know what had happened to fracture Kelsey's family? He didn't want to ask Howard. It was Kelsey's story to tell. He wanted her to tell him if and when she chose. "I'm sorry."

"So am I."

Kelsey shrugged as if it wasn't a big deal. But it was a very big deal. He and his dad lived at opposite ends of the state, yet he couldn't envision that kind of estrangement existing between them. He could tell from her discomfort that she was done talking about the emotional minefield of her father–daughter relationship.

"Tell me about what's happening on the wedding front."

She threw him a grateful smile and plunged into an elaborate narrative—waving hands and all—about the latest Everest-size hurdles she'd overcome for the Big Day.

"… Miss Dot, your Aunt Trudy and I will head to Asheville tomorrow to buy your grandmother's wedding dress. This close to the actual date, it will have to be something on the rack."

"How about I come along as your personal chauffeur?" He retrieved the ax. "If you're interested, that is."

She smiled. "I'm interested."

For the love of mistletoe, him, too. What was he so afraid of? For the duration of the next few weeks, why not just enjoy each other?

After the wedding, she'd return to her real life in Asheville. He'd return to the comforting, normal ranch routine he cherished. But for the first time, the prospect of a Truelove future without her in it didn't seem half so appealing.

Chapter Six

The next morning at breakfast, Kelsey sat at the kitchen table overlooking Martha Alice's garden. Clay was picking her up, along with Miss Dot, soon. His Aunt Trudy, recently promoted to Mason Jar manager, had been unable to join them due to an unforeseen staffing issue, but Kelsey had promised to video everything and get her input on finalizing the bridesmaid dresses.

Kelsey slathered Martha Alice's fig jam on a slice of toast and took a bite.

"Such an exciting day." Martha Alice filled her tea mug with hot water from the electric kettle on the counter. "Last summer, Kate and I had a wonderful time picking out her dress to renew her vows with Jack. Y'all will have such fun."

Kelsey was disappointed the lively, speak-her-mind Trudy wasn't coming. "I hope so."

Ideally, wedding-dress shopping was a mother–daughter endeavor. She took another bite of toast. A sudden thought struck her. With Granna gone, who would shop with her following Kelsey's yet-to-be-determined future engagement? Frowning, she swallowed.

Without Trudy's buffering presence, Kelsey was afraid the trip would get awkward.

"Miss Dot and I don't know each other well..." How could she say this without it sounding like an indictment? "Her tastes and interests are different from mine or Granna's. We don't have much in common."

"Except the most important thing of all—your love for Howard." Her grandmother's best friend set down the mug. "Dorothy is a wonderful woman. She will never be Joan, and she shouldn't have to be anybody but herself."

"I know," Kelsey said in a small voice. "But Grampy always loved Granna's style, and Miss Dot prefers simpler things."

Martha Alice took her hand. "You need to ask yourself who you are planning this wedding for. Are you truly striving to serve Dorothy's wishes or your own?"

Kelsey's bottom lip wobbled. She was trying to please her father, who'd adored his mother. She was being completely unfair to Dorothy.

"Simple doesn't have to mean *lesser*." Martha Alice gestured at the window. "Take the garden, for instance. I love the spring with its profusion of bulbs and the aroma of my roses, but next best of the seasons in my garden I love is winter."

Kelsey flicked a glance out the window. "Why?" She bent her head. "Sorry."

Martha Alice smiled. "You just need to train your eyes better to see what's there versus what's not. It's a matter of perspective."

"I don't understand."

"Take a look again, but this time notice how the evergreen hollies provide a soothing visual structure that ties together the entire enterprise. Note the sharp contrast of the red berries against the framework of green. Oh, look." Martha Alice pointed. "A cardinal just landed on one of the branches. Another joy of winter. During the rest of the year, you can't always see the birds. But with everything stripped away, you can better appreciate the joys of the unexpected."

She'd already experienced joy during the planning of this very unexpected wedding. In the person of Clay McKendry. And even better than the position she hoped to earn in the firm, she and her father were finally communicating.

"Then, there are the trees."

Kelsey followed Martha Alice's gaze out the window.

"Stripped of their leaf finery, there is a stark beauty to the trees, their bare branches lifted to the sky." Martha Alice took a sip of tea. "Simple has a beauty all its own."

The older woman was right. This wedding was Dorothy's day. Not Granna's nor Kelsey's.

She needed to get her priorities straight. It was time to let go of the vision in her head about what Granna would have done. This wasn't about pleasing her father but about celebrating the love Grampy shared with the new woman in his life.

"Thank you, Miss Marth'Alice." She squeezed the older woman's hand. "For the master class in design and for everything else, too."

"You're welcome." At the sound of a vehicle in the driveway, Martha Alice turned her head. "I believe your chariot has arrived. Go have a fantastic day."

Granna wouldn't have been proud of how she'd too often run roughshod over Dorothy's wishes. She sent Clay a quick text to let him know she was on her way out.

Donning her coat, she prayed for God to help her change her attitude toward her soon-to-be new grandmother. And to listen, really listen, to Dorothy's desires.

Kelsey grabbed her purse and left the house. She hoped it wasn't too late to repair her mistakes with Grampy's new bride.

In an attempt to show interest in their world, during the long drive to Asheville, she asked a lot of questions about the cattle business. At one point, Clay's gaze flicked to hers in the rearview mirror. He smiled at her as if he understood what she was trying to do and appreciated her efforts.

He dropped them off at the curb in front of the bridal boutique. "I'm headed to the men's formalwear shop down the block."

She helped Dorothy out of the truck. "Our appointment is for ninety minutes."

"No rush." He looked across the seat through the open window. "I may get a coffee from the double-decker you told me about. You ladies have a fabulous time."

She threw open her hands. "What could be more fun than wedding-dress shopping?"

Frowning, Dorothy pursed her lips. He drove away.

"This looks like a fancy place." His grandmother cast a critical look at the storefront. "I'm not a fancy person."

Kelsey put on a bright, encouraging face. "I'm sure we can find something you like."

"I'm more a casual jeans sort of gal." Dorothy clutched the strap of her purse. "Not much need for folderol on the ranch."

"Why don't we look to see if they have anything that interests you? If not, we'll look somewhere else."

"I don't know why I let you talk me into coming here." Dorothy jutted her jaw. "I hate shopping."

Shopping was one of Kelsey's favorite recreational activities. She and Granna had spent hours shopping together, enjoying each other's company. But Dorothy was not Granna. She had different interests. Kelsey scrambled for a way to save the day.

"I can cancel the appointment with the bridal specialist if there is somewhere else you'd rather shop."

Dorothy harrumphed. "We might as well go in." She motioned toward the Tiffany-blue painted door. "Since we're here." Her hand shook.

Was Miss Dot nervous?

"Everyone is nice here, I promise. But say the word, and I'll have Clay come get us."

A middle-aged sales associate greeted them. The lady, Cynthia, introduced herself to Dorothy. "Is this your granddaughter?"

"No." Dorothy held the strap of her purse on her shoulder. "My family couldn't make it."

Cynthia's smile never wavered, but her gaze flitted to Kelsey before she led them over to a sitting area with a French provincial love seat and wing chairs. On the walls hung elaborate gilded mirrors. With visible reluctance, Dorothy sank onto the cerulean silk settee. Kelsey settled beside her.

"How may I be of assistance today?"

Dorothy held her purse tightly in her lap. "I need to find a wedding dress." Her mouth tightened. "Silly, isn't it? A wedding dress for an old woman like me."

Cynthia leaned forward. "Not silly at all. Every woman should feel special on her wedding day, and we want to do everything we can to make that dream come true." She laid a comforting hand on Dorothy's. "If I might ask a few questions, to get a feel for the style of your wedding… Where, when…?"

"December third." Dorothy remained rigid. "As for the rest…ask her. She's in charge of everything."

Kelsey gave the sales associate a rundown on the details thus far—the winter-wonderland theme, color palette and the name of the resort.

"We've worked with many brides there." Cynthia made

a few notes on an iPad. "Do you have any photos of wedding-dress styles you're interested in, Mrs. McKendry?"

"I don't want a long dress. Too easy to trip on the hem. Don't need to break a hip." Dorothy fidgeted. "I want knee-length and not tight. Howard and I intend to dance."

"We have a wonderful selection of party dresses." Cynthia smiled. "In keeping with the theme, we could start by looking at something glittery and fun."

Kelsey nodded. "That would look wonderful with your lovely silver hair, Miss Dot."

Dorothy touched a gnarled hand to her hair. "You think my hair is lovely?"

Maybe Kelsey wasn't the only one unsure of herself. "Absolutely."

"I'll pull some gowns for you to preview." Cynthia surged to her feet. "Perhaps you'd care to join me, Miss Summerfield?"

She wanted to do right by Miss Dot's wishes, but the problem was prying those preferences out of the older woman. "I'll be there in a minute."

Cynthia disappeared into the back.

She cleared her throat. "When you were a young girl, did you ever dream about the day you'd become a bride?"

Dorothy ran her hand down her slacks. "Clay's grandfather and I were high-school sweethearts. I wanted a church wedding, but Willard was drafted into the army. We eloped to South Carolina a few days before he shipped out to Vietnam. Clay's father, Gary, was born while he was overseas."

"That must've been hard, Miss Dot. To be pregnant and alone."

"It was." Dorothy's eyes became hooded. "But harder still was when Willard came home from the war. He was not the same boy I married."

Kelsey wasn't sure how to respond. She sensed now was the time to listen, though. Really listen.

"He was a difficult man." Dorothy fiddled with a stray thread on her slacks. "He had mood swings. I took over the running of the ranch. Willard was not a good father. He and Gary had a difficult relationship. It's no wonder Gary hated ranching."

"Whereas Clay always loved it?"

A whisper of a smile drifted across her lips. "As a little boy, he took to it right away. Kind of like I did when I came to the Bar None as a young bride." Her mouth drooped. "But as soon as he could get away from the ranch and his father, Gary did. Trudy, too."

"You've made a beautiful home for your family on the ranch."

Dorothy looked at her. "Unlike Howard and Joan, I did not have a fairy-tale marriage. Howard and I are so different." Her chin wobbled.

Kelsey grasped her hand. "Do you love my grandfather, Miss Dot?"

Dorothy's eyes watered. "I do."

"Then, we'll find a dress you love, which positively knocks his socks off."

"At my age, I'm not interested in a white dress, although that's fine for some." The older woman ran a finger under her eyeglasses. "To answer your question—as a young girl, I always imagined myself in lace."

Giving her a smile, Kelsey rose. "Let's see what Cynthia and I can find."

Heading for the area behind the dressing rooms, she met Cynthia coming out with an armload full of gowns.

"What do you think?"

Kelsey gave them the once-over. They were exactly the kind of dresses that fit perfectly with her wedding design.

The sort of gowns Granna herself would have chosen and worn. Sparkling with sequins. Glittering with rhinestones. But not Dorothy's style.

She put her finger on her chin. "Do you have any silver dresses in lace?"

Cynthia cocked her head. "I might have the perfect thing for your grandmother."

"Dorothy's not—" Adjusting her attitude, Kelsey closed her mouth.

Soon after, Cynthia settled Dorothy into a dressing room. Kelsey waited outside while Cynthia assisted Dorothy into one of the gowns she'd pulled. Moments later, Dorothy emerged in her stocking feet. Kelsey's breath caught.

With a matching silver lace jacket, the lacy sheath dress was sleeveless. The knee-length hem was scalloped, matching the scalloped lace trim on the jacket. The ensemble was comfortable and elegant.

She clasped her hands together. "Oh, Miss Dot. You look beautiful."

Cynthia led the older woman to a low dais, surrounded on three sides by mirrors. Dorothy plucked at the three-quarter-length sleeve. "You don't think I look too frou-frou?"

"You look gorgeous." She smiled at the older woman's reflection in the mirror. "It shows off how slender and willowy you are. I've always wanted to be willowy. But at my height? Not happening."

Dorothy turned this way and that, getting a glimpse from every angle. "It does look right nice on me. I feel like a fairy-tale princess."

Kelsey and Cynthia exchanged a smile.

"It only needs one more thing to be perfect."

Cynthia stepped forward. "What's that, Mrs. McKendry?"

"Shoes." Dorothy smiled. "I want some of those Cinderella slippers. The more shimmery, the better."

For safety and comfort, Cynthia showed Dorothy several options that included a low block heel. Dorothy chose a glittery, closed-toe shoe with a large rhinestone-bow embellishment.

"Don't I look fancy." Dorothy admired herself in the mirror. "Maybe fancy isn't as bad as I believed it would be." She turned around. "What should I put in my hair? What about a hat?"

Ultimately, Dorothy chose a silver mesh fascinator with small feathers, chiffon ribbon and birdcage veiling. She clipped it onto the side of her head and stood back to admire the effect.

"Very vintage," Cynthia cooed.

"I'm more antique than vintage." Dorothy laughed. "Kelsey, what do you think?"

She smiled. "It's the perfect touch. Glamorous, sassy and trendy."

"I've had the *sassy* part down for years." Dorothy fluttered her hand. "Never been called *glamorous* or *trendy* before, though."

The bell over the door at the entrance jangled.

"Am I too late?" Trudy swept in. "Oh, Mama. Don't you look a treat!"

Dorothy held her hand out to her daughter. "I thought you had to work."

"Crisis averted, and I drove here fast as the law allowed." Trudy stepped onto the dais and gave her a hug. "I wouldn't miss this for the world."

"I'm glad you're here, honey." Dorothy reached for Kelsey to join them. "But Kelsey and Cindy have taken good care of me."

Cynthia winked at Kelsey.

"I'm gonna take a load off my feet and sit down. Trudy, you girls sort out the bridesmaid dresses. Kelsey wants something blue."

Cynthia's assistant, a younger girl in training, whisked Dorothy to the sitting area. With Cynthia in tow, Trudy headed toward the storeroom. Kelsey felt a frisson of concern.

Trudy's fashion style tended toward what Granna would have kindly referred to as *vibrantly eclectic*. Kelsey reminded herself to stop being such a control freak. She let Trudy enjoy sifting through the inventory.

And braced to wear whatever Trudy selected without complaint.

With several garments in her arms, Cynthia returned to the dressing area first. Trudy sashayed from behind the curtain and held up the gaudiest dress Kelsey had ever beheld in her life. "What do you think of this one?" She grinned. "You wanted blue, right?"

Kelsey flinched before she caught herself.

Aka Vegas showgirl, the orange-and-blue bedazzled gown glimmered under the lighting of the crystal chandelier. And then there was the white feather boa that apparently completed the ensemble.

"I-I…" Kelsey gulped. "It's very…very eye-catching."

Trudy burst out laughing. "If you could see your face… I was just funnin' you." She handed the dress to the assistant. "Cindy has the real dresses I picked out. See what you think."

Clay's aunt had chosen a velvet gown in a rich shade of blue with violet undertones. Each of the five dresses was a slight variation on the others. They were glorious.

"I'm partial to the one with the halter top." Trudy held the dress against her body. "Shows off those sculpted arms I've got from lifting trays all day." She curled her bicep.

"I'll let my niece, Rebecca, pick one from among these three. But for you? This one has your name on it."

Cynthia held the hanger out to Kelsey.

"Try it on," Trudy urged. "I'll put on mine, and we'll give Mama a fashion show."

Inside the dressing room, Kelsey changed into the floor-length gown and surveyed the effect in the long gilt mirror. With a sweeping train and sheer beaded short sleeves, the dress had a V-neckline, exposing her shoulders. *Wow.* Trudy had somehow managed to completely capture the vibe Kelsey was aiming for with the wedding.

Would Clay like her in it? She flushed, annoyed with herself. What did it matter if he liked her in it or not? She liked herself in it. As long as Miss Dot was happy, she was happy.

"So…what do you think?" Trudy called through the curtain.

"You did good." She ran her hand across the butter-soft velvet of the bodice. "Real good."

"Cindy's found to-die-for shoes," Trudy hollered.

She choked back a laugh.

"Can I come in? I've got an idea for your hair." Trudy bustled in. "I'm thinking French twist for my own do. So classic." Somehow, she quickly wrangled Kelsey's long tresses into a rough facsimile of a bun. She placed a pearl comb set in silver at the base of the chignon. "Imagine what I could do with proper tools."

They stood back to examine themselves.

"I love it," she whispered.

Trudy gave Kelsey a small squeeze. "What's not to love?"

Chapter Seven

As Clay pushed into the bridal boutique, a bell jangled overhead. Ninety minutes had stretched into two hours, but he didn't mind. After being fitted for his suit, he'd stopped by the double-decker for coffee. Nana had texted him to come to the shop. She wanted to show him her dress.

Hat in hand, he stood at the entrance, feeling out of place amidst the frippery. A college-age girl ushered him into a sitting area. Nana rose.

A lump settled in his throat. "Well, look at you."

Nana Dot threw him a small smile. "You like?"

"Simply spectacular." He made a whirling motion with his finger. "Give it a turn. Let me get a gander at the whole package."

With an uncharacteristic girlish giggle, she did a slow three-sixty. He kissed her cheek. She had enjoyed herself. *Thank you, Keltz.*

"Have a seat." She patted the cushion beside her on the love seat. "Trudy made it here after all." She touched the totally feminine, frothy concoction perched on the side of her head. "Kelsey is a wonder. The girl has incredible taste. Guess how I know."

"The hat."

"Nope."

Clay chuckled. "The dress?"

Nana shook her head.

"The shoes."

"Wrong." Nana threw him a pert grin. "She has incredible taste because she likes you. And you like her, too."

"Nana," he sputtered.

"Don't bother denying it." She wagged her finger. "I know it's true 'cause y'all have all the signs."

"Signs of what?"

"Don't be coy, Clayton." His grandmother's eyebrow arched. "It doesn't become a cowboy."

"Nana," he grunted.

"I've seen the way you light up every time she walks in a room. The long glances between you. You only have eyes for each other."

"How can you say that?" He stared at her. "We're like oil and water. Night and day. We argue all the time."

"Spark to kindling." She snapped her fingers. "Match to dynamite."

"Combustible substances shouldn't mix."

"You're fooling no one with your little differences of opinion. It's clear as the nose on your face you two amuse each other no end."

He winced at the *you two*.

She gave him a look. "I'm not the only one who's noticed."

"Please tell me the matchmakers aren't involved," he moaned.

"What you call *combustion*, GeorgeAnne and I call *chemistry*."

Groaning, he dropped his head into his hands.

Trudy stepped into the sitting area. "Howdy, nephew. What do you think? Mama?"

Clay stood.

Holding his chin between his thumb and forefinger, he frowned. "I'm afraid I can't allow you to appear in public in this getup."

Trudy's eyes widened. "What's wrong with the dress?"

"Nothing, except you're so gorgeous you'll take the focus off the bride."

His grandmother laughed.

Trudy gave him a peck on the cheek. "This is why you're my favorite nephew."

"I'm your only nephew."

"Doesn't make it any less true." She motioned him and Nana back to the love seat. "Kelsey?" she called. "Your turn. Come out here."

Nana leaned close. "Better not let this one get away. There's not many like Kelsey Summerfield."

She stepped through the curtain. His heart almost stopped from the sheer loveliness of her.

"Oh, Clay." Blushing, her eyes met his, darted away and found his gaze again. "I didn't expect to see you here."

The elegant dress was almost the exact color of her eyes. The neckline exposed her creamy shoulders. He'd never seen her hair off her neck. He liked her hair up.

His gaze traveled to the vein pulsing at the hollow of her neck. If she was this magnificent in blue, what would she look like in white as a bride? Something turned over in his chest. Their eyes locked.

For a split second it was as if everything and everyone else in the universe ceased to exist.

His aunt snapped her fingers in front of his face. "Earth to Clay."

Clay jolted, suddenly aware she'd probably been trying to get his attention for some time. "What?" He shifted.

"I said, how do you think Kelsey looks in her gown?"

Cheeks burning, he turned the hat in his hands. Caught off guard, no way could he say what actually rose to his mind—stunning, mind-blowing, world-shattering. "It's nice."

Kelsey's smile dropped. His aunt made a disgusted noise in the back of her throat. Nana shook her head.

"I'll change." Turning on her stiletto heel, Kelsey dashed behind the curtain.

Trudy rushed after her. "Men," she said and sniffed.

Nana's look of reproach left him squirming. "I should change out of my wedding duds, too. Then settle up with the shop."

When the ladies rejoined him, Kelsey gave him the cold shoulder. He twisted his hat in his hands.

The shop lady tallied their purchases. Shoes. Hats. The younger girl boxed up the items. He counted two dress boxes.

"Keltz?"

Ignoring him, she gave the wall behind the register her undivided attention.

"You're buying the dress, aren't you?"

"What do you care?" She gritted her teeth. "I didn't think you liked me in that dress." She crossed her arms.

"I love you in that dress."

Her eyes flitted to his.

"You took my breath." He put his hat over his heart. "The sight of you robbed me of words. Say you're buying it."

She propped her hands on her hips. "Just so we're clear, *if* I buy it, it will be because it works with the wedding theme and because I like it."

"Of course." One of these days, he was going to lose the war waging within himself and kiss her. He dropped his gaze to her mouth. Most probably sooner, not later.

"You'd never buy a dress just because in it I think you're the most gorgeous woman I've ever seen."

"Absolutely not." Her mouth curved. "But it's nice to hear you say you like it."

The dress wasn't all he liked. All of a sudden, he wasn't ready for the day to end.

"How about we send Nana Dot back to Truelove with Aunt Trudy?"

Kelsey gave him a look out of the corner of her eye. "Why, pray tell, would we do that?"

"Spend the day with me, City Girl. Show me your town. Besides," he shuffled his feet, "I've got a hankering for sushi."

"Okay." She smiled. "Since there isn't any sushi in Truelove."

No, there wasn't. And after the wedding was over, there'd be no Kelsey either.

The smart thing to do would be to stick to his arm's-length policy. But when it came to Kelsey Summerfield, he'd already proven smart wasn't his fallback. It wasn't like they were going to fall in love or anything stupid like that.

Night and day. Fire and ice. Spark to kindling...

His grandmother made arrangements for Clay's sister, Rebecca, to visit the shop in a few days. The lady at the register handed the packages to Trudy. "This has been one of the most enjoyable appointments I've ever done."

Nana hugged Kelsey. "It has been fun, hasn't it?"

Trudy thrust a box at him. "You think this is fun, wait till I kick up my heels at the reception."

He walked them to Trudy's car. When he announced their intention to stay in Asheville a bit longer, Nana gave him a knowing smirk.

The next few hours passed in a blur of laughter. They ate lunch at the iconic Woolworth's Soda Fountain. Kelsey gave him a walking tour of Asheville's famed Pack Square and the architecturally rich Art Deco downtown. They drove to the River Arts warehouse district. They strolled around converted studios where a range of artisans performed glassblowing, threw pottery and demonstrated wood carving.

Sometime during the walking tour, Kelsey's hand found her way into his. At a lower elevation, Asheville didn't get the snow the Blue Ridge Highlands and Truelove experienced. But it was windy and chilly as befitted a mountain day in November.

Or that was the excuse he gave himself for holding her hand. No day, however, was too chilly in his opinion for ice cream. She took him to her favorite ice cream parlor.

They talked about their childhoods. He was struck as much by what she didn't say as what she did when she talked about that time in her life. They discussed their respective university experiences. No surprise their schools were college rivals.

He broadened his shoulders. "Betcha didn't figure this guy for an agribusiness grad."

"Way to go, Cowboy." She play punched his bicep. "You're smarter than you look."

Later, she told him about what Nana had revealed about his grandfather, Willard.

"He died before I was born." Clay blew out a breath of air. "Nana loved him as much as he allowed her to, but when he died I think it was a relief for her."

Her face grew pensive. "How did it affect your dad?" Was she thinking of her father?

"My dad had no real example for being a husband or father. But he gave it everything he had and then some. He made sure Rebecca and I never suffered for what he himself had lacked."

"That's admirable."

Clay nodded. "He'd tell you he was only able to do it because of my mom's faith in him and his faith in God."

"Your parents sound remarkable."

He smiled. "I've been blessed, but every family has its struggles."

"What about your Aunt Trudy?"

His smile faded. "Nana would say Aunt Trudy went looking for love in all the wrong places. She was hurt badly by her jerk of an ex-husband. She's been single a long time now. I think she keeps it light with men friends for fear of getting hurt again."

"Is that how you feel since Angela—"

"What about you?" His ex-fiancée wasn't a topic he wanted to discuss. Hunching over the table at the ice cream parlor, he stuffed his hands in his coat pockets. "Will you bring a plus-one to the wedding?"

She shrugged. "I hadn't planned on it. I dated a guy during college. He was in a fraternity. We were quite the couple in those days."

Clay experienced a sharp, and hitherto unrealized, antipathy for frat boys.

"I think Grampy would've liked it to become serious."

"But it didn't?" he rasped. "Why not?"

"I wasn't in love with him." She tilted her head. "I'm sorry Angela hurt you."

Up until this conversation, he hadn't been thinking about Angela. He couldn't remember the last time he'd thought of Angela at all. Upon further recollection, perhaps not since City Girl blew into Truelove.

She got to her feet. "Shall we get sushi before the line gets long?"

"You just had ice cream, Summerfield."

She cocked her head. "So you're not hungry?"

He rose. "I can always eat, darlin'."

By the time they finished eating and left the Thai restaurant, darkness had fallen.

Kelsey tugged on his arm. "What would you say about making a small detour before we head to Truelove?"

"Sure. What do you have in mind?"

"There's the Winter Lights display at the arboretum. I could show you where I got some of my ideas for the wedding."

He shook his head. "Does that brain of yours ever take a vacation from wedding planning?"

"Can't afford to take a vacation." She grinned at him. "Not until after this winter extravaganza—"

"Also known as Nana's wedding," he interjected.

She smiled. "Not until Nana Dot's *winter wedding extravaganza* reaches its happily-ever-after conclusion. Actually, I sort of like organizing the details. Apparently, one of the few things I am good at."

He frowned. "That can't be true. Who told you that?"

"Which time?"

"Keltz…"

"No, it's okay. He was right."

Something told Clay she meant her father.

Kelsey linked her arm through his. "I wasn't cut out for law school."

His brow creased. "You went to law school?"

"I attended only a semester before I decided it wasn't for me, much to Dad's disappointment." She hugged his arm. "But I'm really enjoying the wedding prep. Maybe by accident, I've stumbled onto a new career."

At the arboretum, they joined the other couples and families strolling through the gardens, enjoying the light show. She pointed out the uplighting on the birch trees.

He got a better understanding of her plan. Which wasn't as over-the-top as he'd feared.

Nana's wedding in Kelsey's capable hands was shaping up to be a truly magical winter wonderland. As for his heart?

He watched the play of colors flash across her face. By the time this wedding was over and done, he wasn't sure just what shape his heart would be in.

It was only later, much later, as he lay in bed thinking about their day together, he realized he'd called her *darlin'*.

Chapter Eight

Clay drove her home to Truelove.

When had she started thinking about Truelove as home? She'd spent the entire day showing him the only town she'd ever called home.

It was late when they arrived back. It had been the most wonderful of days, but she was glad Martha Alice hadn't waited up. She wasn't ready for questions about her hard-to-define, non-you-two relationship with a certain Truelove cowboy. Clay walked her to the door. She thought—hoped—he might end the evening with a kiss, but he didn't. Probably just as well.

Tumbling into bed, she remembered she hadn't updated her father in a few days. She sent him a brief text about the successful shopping expedition and the info to get his tuxedo fitted. Almost as an afterthought, she mentioned she'd booked a venue.

Immediately, squiggly dots erupted. Where?

She smiled. It was wonderful Dad was taking such a keen interest in this project. She replied, typing in the name of the resort.

Yawning, she shut off her phone. Surely her impossible-to-impress father would be pleased with her efforts.

Over the next week, she went to the ranch several times. Clay put her to work shoveling cow stalls. She didn't mind. She just enjoyed spending time with him at the ranch. They also fell into the habit of going to lunch at the Jar. A working lunch.

Wedding plans were at the forefront of their conversations but not all they talked about.

They were sharing a piece of chocolate chess pie when a shadow fell over the booth. Forks poised over the plate, they looked up. GeorgeAnne Allen loomed over them.

Kelsey pasted on an insincere smile. "Is there anything I can do for you, Miss GeorgeAnne?"

"I'm here to help you." The older woman pointed a bony finger at them. "I hear you two," she said, and Clay blanched, "are in charge of planning Dot and Howard's pending nuptials. It's a big undertaking. The Double Name Club wants to volunteer our services."

Clay studied the salt and pepper shakers with apparent fascination.

"While that is so thoughtful of you, Miss GeorgeAnne—" determinedly positive, she marshaled social niceties around her like a Teflon shield "—we have everything completely under control."

GeorgeAnne's ice-blue eyes narrowed. "The McKendrys are one of the founding families of Truelove. We feel it's important to utilize as much of our local talent as possible. Like Kara, who's ventured into catering."

"Kara's food is excellent, but the resort has in-house caterers." She lifted her chin. "They have everything completely under control."

GeorgeAnne gave her a curt nod. "I have other helpful suggestions."

She gritted her teeth. *Nosy, interfering busybody...* Kelsey folded her arms.

GeorgeAnne widened her stance. "Callie Jackson of Apple Valley Orchard is a photogra—"

"The resort has a photographer on staff."

GeorgeAnne arched a look at her, which probably quailed lesser individuals. Kelsey was not a lesser individual. "Coach Lovett's daughter makes the most beautiful cakes."

"The resort has everything completely—"

"Clay?" GeorgeAnne's thin lips pressed together. "Have you got anything to say for yourself?"

"Yes, Clay." Kelsey skewered him with her eyes. "Is there something you wanted to say?"

His gaze pinged between them. "No, ma'am."

GeorgeAnne sniffed. "If you two decide you need our help, you know where to find us."

At *you two*, Clay's leg underneath the table jiggled.

She bestowed on the older woman a variation of Granna's most gracious smile. "Thank you for your input, Miss GeorgeAnne. I will certainly keep your *suggestions* in mind. You have a good day, now."

The matchmaker exited the Jar with an angry jangling of the bell over the door.

Clay collapsed against the red vinyl seat. "Have you lost your mind?"

She blew out a breath. "I will not be bullied by the likes of GeorgeAnne Allen."

He shook his head. "For the love of Christmas, what were you thinking? Don't poke the bear."

She stabbed the pie with her fork. "You don't have to run faster than the bear, Clay. You just have to run faster than the guy next to you."

"Which would be me." He glared. "When they have me lassoed and hitched by spring, I'll have you to thank."

She laughed. "Lassoed and hitched?"

He pointed his fork at her. "Maddie Lovett makes the

best cakes on earth. She freelances bakery and dessert items for the Jar. You're eating one of her pies right now."

"It's fabulous, but the resort already—"

"Has everything under control. Got it." He shook his head. "Way to put a target on both our backs, City Girl."

The next day, Clay's friend, Sam Gibson, and his wife, Lila, joined them for lunch. They remembered Kelsey from the wedding of their mutual friend at the resort.

Lila had the loveliest curly red hair. She was a renowned landscape artist at Ashmont College. Bubbly and energetic, she also ran a visual-arts program for underserved children in the mountains. Her face glowed when she talked about Emma Cate, Sam's seven-year-old niece whom they'd adopted. Kelsey looked forward to meeting her.

Although, once Grampy was married, she wasn't sure how often she'd have the chance to visit Truelove. Her life would be firmly fixed in Asheville and her new position within the Summerfield company. Her gaze drifted to Clay talking football with Sam.

The idea of returning to the city didn't thrill her as much as she would have supposed. Nor the potential job within her father's company she'd dreamed of. She'd always wanted a seat at the Summerfield table. But now maybe not.

Perhaps the dream wasn't really about sitting at the Summerfield table but more about sitting at her father's table. She was beginning to believe she wasn't suited for the cutthroat commercial real-estate market. But what else was she good at?

Weddings?

Clay left to install a new wood stove in the calving barn so the winter-born calves would have a warm place to gain strength before heading into the corrals. Kelsey suppressed a small sigh. She'd see him tomorrow, but she missed him already.

Lila inched out of the booth. "You got it bad, girl."

"I absolutely do not!"

Sam reached for the check on the table. "My ole buddy looks to have it pretty bad, too."

Her pulse quickened. Did Clay really look at her that way?

Sam insisted on paying for Kelsey's lunch. She and Lila ambled onto the sidewalk to wait for him.

Lila smiled at her. "How are you finding Truelove? Different from what you're used to, I imagine."

"It's a slower pace, for sure." With the leaves completely off the trees, she spotted an intriguing glint of metal high atop one of the mountain peaks overlooking the small hamlet. "But I'm beginning to think slower might suit me."

Her gaze traced the rounded outline of the gleaming roof, and she pointed. "Would you happen to know what that is up there?"

Lila peered into the distance. "That's probably the old Birchfield place on Laurel Mountain Road. In its heyday, it was quite the showplace, I understand. Of course, the Birchfields are long gone. Timber barons."

"Who lives there now?"

Lila shrugged. "Maybe nobody. I don't know. At one point, a historic preservation group had it restored and sold it to the college, but it was never utilized to its full potential. I think the upkeep became too much."

Sam came out of the Jar. They said goodbye. At loose ends, she wasn't sure what to do this afternoon.

But, her curiosity piqued, her gaze drifted toward the glimmering mansion overlooking the town. Why not see it for herself? Adventure beckoned.

She plugged *Birchfield* on Laurel Mountain Road into her cell. Following the GPS, she drove over the bridge and out of town. She continued past the steepled white-clapboard church she'd attended last Sunday with Martha Alice.

The road climbed, winding upward. Towering evergreen mountain laurel hugged both sides of the road. A quarter of a mile off the road, she came upon two enormous stone pillars, inscribed with *Birchfield*. This was the place.

She parked to the side of a curving drive that disappeared into the trees. She took the partially open scrolled-iron gate as an invitation. On foot, she followed the driveway another quarter of a mile. Trudging along, she was glad she'd worn the low-heel knee boots instead of her fashionably painful ones. Her breath puffed in the crisp coldness of the late-November afternoon.

A sane person would think twice before trespassing on private property. A caretaker might run her off with a shotgun. Or there could be guard dogs.

That stopped her in her tracks.

Her heart pounded in her chest. Ahead, the tree line widened. Despite her reservations, something drove her on. At the top of the incline, she emerged into a clearing.

She gasped.

The house—*what a house!*—perched on a knoll. Like an English country manor, the sprawling three-story mansion sparkled like an exquisite jewel. Taking out her phone, she snapped a picture. Unable to resist, she stood on the porch, hands framing her eyes, peering through the glass panels surrounding the massive oak door to see what she could of the interior.

What she glimpsed was impressive. Beyond the door lay an enormous foyer from which the east and west wings of the house branched off. The grand staircase was breathtaking.

She followed a stone path around the house, peeking

into as many windows as she could. She did a complete circuit of the house. French doors opened onto a series of stone terraces.

Kelsey explored the grounds. Low stone walls enclosed overgrown, once-spectacular gardens. At the bottom of the slope she found a stone gazebo on a level piece of ground. A perfect spot for a wedding. With that grand staircase and the large open spaces inside the house for gatherings, the entire estate was a wedding-venue dream. Tons of natural light.

A kernel of an idea popped into her brain.

Climbing back to the top terrace, she was struck by the panoramic grandeur of the mountain horizon. Far below, she spied the glinting silver of the river. Beyond the small hamlet, dappled fields and orchards rounded out the patchwork kingdom of tiny Truelove.

From the slanting light of the sun through the trees, she became aware the afternoon was nearly gone. The estate was isolated. No one knew where she was. If something was to happen…

She rounded the corner of the house to find a silver BMW parked in the circle drive. Was someone inside the house? Friend or foe?

Questioning the dubious wisdom of several recent-life choices, she was slinking past the car when a voice called from the porch.

"Who are you, and what do you think you're doing here?"

She froze. Shotgun and canine scenarios floated across her brain. Her pulse quickened. Gulping, she pivoted.

A trim, well-appointed blonde woman in her late forties stood on the steps. Dressed in a skirt and suit coat, she wore the kind of high-heeled dressy boots Kelsey would've bought. If she wasn't about to go to jail or get shot or have dogs set upon her.

The woman's carefully made-up face went from a frown to a smile. "I recognize you from the Jar. You're Kelsey Summerfield, staying with Miss Marth'Alice." Bridging the distance between them, she extended her hand. "I'm Mary Sue Ingersoll, the listing agent for this property."

Her heart slowed to a more natural rhythm. She'd seen the realtor's face plastered on a highway billboard between Truelove and Asheville. Mary Sue Ingersoll ran a real-estate agency, the only one in Truelove.

She shook the woman's hand. "I shouldn't have wandered in, but the gate was open, and I couldn't resist."

"It's something, isn't it? Built in 1925 as the mountain getaway for the prominent Birchfield family."

Kelsey studied the house. "It's magnificent. Imagine the parties and the people who probably once strolled this lawn." She flung out her hand. "Chinese lanterns. Fringed dresses. Pin-striped suits."

Mary Sue chuckled. "Very *Gatsby*. Several presidents, including Hoover, dined here over the years. It's said a silent-film actress also lived here for a while. While the Birchfields managed to survive the stock-market crash, they couldn't outwit time. Ten years ago, the last of them died without heirs. It's been lovingly restored by a local heritage society and includes most of the original furnishings."

"It's an architectural treasure."

"Three acres. Seventy-five hundred square feet." Mary Sue tilted her head. "Lots of possibilities. Your family develops commercial properties. Care to make an offer?"

"Don't I wish." She sighed. "My father develops property, not me. Million-dollar view. Million-dollar price tag."

Mary Sue coughed gently into her hand. "Try again. But round up a mil."

She cast one last, longing look at the house. "So much potential but well out of my reach."

Mary Sue handed her a business card. "It doesn't hurt to dream."

The image of a certain cowboy flitted across her mind, and her heart skipped a beat.

At the Mason Jar, Clay only half listened as Kelsey went over—for the umpteenth time—her to-do list. His mind ought to be focused on Nana's wedding or at least his current winter project of leveling the dirt in the corral in advance of the winter birthing season.

But despite daily admonishments to get it together, he spent most nights counting the hours until he saw Kelsey again. Pretty pathetic for a cowboy who'd renounced romantic entanglements.

He was entangled all right. He stirred cream into his coffee. Kelsey Summerfield drank more coffee than anyone he'd ever known. Must be where she got her energy from. Judging from her bright eyes and the sparkling smile she flashed his way, nothing appeared to keep her up at night, including him.

"... Per the seating charts I've created—"

"For the love of Christmas, Keltz, take a breath."

"Boring you, am I, Clayton?"

"You are the least boring person I know." Clanging the spoon against the white porcelain mug, he frowned. "But could we talk about anything other than wedding stuff?"

She closed her laptop. Her elaborate, step-by-step, day-of plans might not have been out of place at the invasion of Normandy. "What would you like to talk about?"

"I'm always up for talking about food."

She rolled her eyes. "Is food all you ever think about?"

As a matter of fact, food wasn't all he thought about. Spending time with Kelsey dominated most of his thoughts.

"I don't know where you put the food."

He shrugged. "It's my long legs. They're hollow."

Their gazes locked. His lips twitched.

She burst out laughing. "You are so ridiculous, McKendry."

He grinned. He'd made it his personal mission to make her laugh every day. His phone beeped with an incoming text.

"Nana says the jeweler has finished sizing their wedding rings. Asks if one of us could pick 'em up for her. Save her a trip to town."

Kelsey grabbed hold of the edge of the table. "Will do."

"Hold on to your stilettos there, City Girl." He replied to the text. "Makes more sense for me to take them to the ranch." He glanced up. "No reason we both can't go to the store, though." No reason he should turn down spending more time with her.

She smiled. "Great." She took hold of the table again as if to slingshot her way out of the booth.

"But—" he checked the time "—the jewelry-store owner goes home for lunch and doesn't reopen the store again until one o'clock each day. We've got a few minutes."

"You know this how?"

"Everybody in Truelove knows this. Exact same schedule for decades."

She smiled. "Small-town charm at its finest."

He loved his hometown, but he was beginning to appreciate the advantages only the city offered. Namely, the vivacious brunette sitting across from him. "Real tree or fake?"

Kelsey's mouth curved. "I prefer real."

"Me, too. There may be hope for you yet." He planted

his elbows on the table. "I'm learning not to be surprised by anything that concerns you."

"Smart man. Christmas dinner or dessert?"

He cocked his head. "What do you think?"

"Both."

He chuckled. "Nailed it in one."

"Where do you see yourself in five years, Cowboy?"

"The Bar None. McKendrys have ranched that land since the Civil War. It's a legacy I don't take lightly." He cut his gaze out the window overlooking the square. "This'll probably sound lame, but it comes down to faith, family and home for me."

"Sounds pretty wonderful to me."

His eyes flitted to hers. "There you go surprising me again. What dreams are you dreaming?"

"A couple of weeks ago, I believed I had my future mapped out, but now?" She sighed. "I'm not sure where I belong or if the thing I wanted most is the right path for me." She grabbed her phone. "Let me show you what I found yesterday." She held it out for him to view the pictures she'd taken. "Birchfield. Have you ever been there?"

"I don't think so."

"A fabulous place for a wedding venue. Don't you think?"

He took the phone from her and enlarged one of the photos. "What are you thinking?"

"I've had the craziest idea ever… There aren't any event venues close to Truelove. Imagine the jobs something like this could bring and the boost to the local economy."

He continued to scroll through her pictures.

"Am I crazy? Tell me I'm crazy to even contemplate an enterprise of this magnitude."

"You're crazy." He handed back her cell. "But you've taken like a horse to a sugar cube with this whole wedding thing. You have experience planning events for your father."

"True." Shaking her head, she leaned back. "But the financial investment alone…"

"If anyone could make it happen, Keltz, it's you."

She looked at him. "I've decided to hire Maddie Lovett here in Truelove to do the wedding cake."

He smiled. "Thanks for giving her a chance. You won't be disappointed with the results." He glanced at his watch. "Let's go pick out—I mean pick up the rings." Flushing, he got out of the booth.

Outside the jewelry store, she became entranced with the twinkling, miniature village of Truelove displayed in the front window. She oohed and aahed, locating the Mason Jar first and then Martha Alice's neighborhood.

The things that delighted Kelsey Summerfield never failed to amaze him.

Grinning, he dragged her inside the store.

While the jeweler disappeared into the storeroom to retrieve the wedding rings, he noticed Kelsey had wandered over to a section featuring antique estate jewelry.

"I had you figured for a thoroughly modern, all-about-the-bling sort of gal."

His assumption was based entirely on the fact she was a Summerfield. However, he'd never seen her wear much jewelry, other than a watch and various pairs of earrings. Nothing too over-the-top. Maybe she saved the expensive stuff for special occasions when she got glammed up.

Kelsey's gaze trailed along the glass case. "I like old things." She nudged him with her shoulder. "It's why I hang out with you."

She made him sound ancient. "Three years' difference is hardly worth mentioning."

The jeweler returned with the wedding bands, boxed

and bagged. When Clay turned around again, once more her attention had become ensnared by the estate jewelry case.

He rejoined her. "Why old things, Keltz?"

She winked. "Because you're funny and a ginger and—"

"Ha. Ha. Ha."

"I admire the workmanship and the artistry." She shrugged. "I like to imagine the happy stories each piece could tell."

He wrinkled his brow. "Not every story has a happy ending."

"In my dreams, they do."

He set the bag on top of the case. "Which one speaks happily-ever-after to you?"

Fluttering her hands, she backed away. "This is silly. We should go." She tugged at his arm.

"Show me, Kelsey. I'd like to know."

Bending over the case, she pointed.

He signaled the jeweler. "Could she try on one of the pieces in here?"

Unlocking the case, the jeweler plucked out the understated sapphire ring. Two smaller diamonds rode sidesaddle. The fretwork was intricate and classy. It was so her.

The jeweler handed it to her. "A lovely little ring from the 1920s. Very Art Deco."

She slipped the ring on her finger. A perfect fit. "I love Art Deco." She moved her hand this way and that, catching the light, setting the sparkle free.

He took hold of her hand to admire the effect. They smiled at each other. He felt a gust of cold air. Someone entered the shop. He turned.

Framed in the doorway, like a gargoyle gone wrong, GeorgeAnne Allen smirked. "What are you two up to now?" She eyeballed them. "The cowboy finally takes a wife."

He dropped Kelsey's hand. Simultaneously, they backed away from each other. Her cheeks scarlet, Kelsey tore the ring off her finger and thrust it at the jeweler.

"It's not what it looks like," he stammered.

GeorgeAnne gloated. "Of course it isn't."

Kelsey waved her hand, now minus the vintage ring. "We were just picking up Grampy and Dorothy's wedding bands."

"Sure you were."

He seized the bag and held it up as evidence.

Kelsey edged around the older woman. "Marth'Alice is probably wondering where I am. Bye." *Sorry*, she mouthed to him from behind GeorgeAnne's back. Fleeing, she slipped out the door. Leaving him to slay the dragon alone.

"We weren't…" He gulped. "We aren't…"

GeorgeAnne gave him a supercilious smile. "Your secret is safe with me."

He understood what that meant all too well. He beat a hasty retreat. Outside on the sidewalk, he sucked in a lungful of air.

She'd have his grandmother on speed dial within seconds. ErmaJean, IdaLee and Martha Alice would be next on her call list. By the time rumors about another, imminent engagement finished making the rounds, the Truelove grapevine would have them roped and steered into wedded bliss by the New Year.

Yet despite his worst nightmare come true, being the other half of a *you two* with Kelsey might not be as bad as he'd feared. Heading to his truck, he hummed "It Came upon the Midnight Clear."

Since he'd met Kelsey, his life had become a lot more interesting. And fun.

Chapter Nine

On Tuesday, Kelsey drove Dorothy to the bridal boutique in Asheville. Cynthia greeted them like long-lost friends. They were meeting Miss Dot's granddaughter, Rebecca, so she could be fitted for her bridesmaid dress. Kelsey was nervous about meeting Clay's sister, but the young mother of two couldn't have been friendlier.

Kelsey saw the resemblance between Clay and his sister. Including the supposedly not-red color of their hair.

"I love my children dearly." On the dais in her gown, Rebecca did a slow twirl in front of the mirror. "But I can't tell you how much I appreciated the long, *quiet* drive from Boone to Asheville by myself." Her husband, a forest ranger, had taken a half day off to keep the kids.

The alterations were minor. Her dress on a hanger, Rebecca was soon ready to depart for her two-hour trek home. She hugged her grandmother. "Next time I see you, Nana, it will be at your wedding."

Nearly lunchtime, Kelsey took Clay's grandmother to one of her and Granna's favorite tearooms. "The chicken salad is the best I've ever eaten."

"That's what I'll order." Dorothy scanned the cozy, Eng-

"One Minute" Survey

GET YOUR FREE BOOKS AND A FREE GIFT!

✓ Complete this Survey ✓ Return this survey

1 Do you try to find time to read every day?

☐ YES ☐ NO

2 Do you prefer books which reflect Christian values?

☐ YES ☐ NO

3 Do you enjoy having books delivered to your home?

☐ YES ☐ NO

4 Do you share your favorite books with friends?

☐ YES ☐ NO

YES! I have completed the above "One Minute" Survey. Please send me my Free Books and a Free Mystery Gift (worth over $20 retail). I understand that I am under no obligation to buy anything, as explained on the back of this card.

☐ **Love Inspired®**
Romance
Larger-Print
122/322 CTI G2AK

☐ **Love Inspired®**
Suspense
Larger-Print
107/307 CTI G2AK

☐ **BOTH**
122/322 & 107/307
CTI G2AL

FIRST NAME

LAST NAME

ADDRESS

APT.#

CITY

STATE/PROV.

ZIP/POSTAL CODE

EMAIL ☐ Please check this box if you would like to receive newsletters and promotional emails from Harlequin Enterprises ULC and its affiliates. You can unsubscribe anytime.

LI/LIS-1123-OM

lish chintz decor. "Such a lovely spot. I've never been here before, but of course it's not often I get into Asheville."

Kelsey poured the older woman a cup of steaming Earl Grey.

Dorothy stirred a lump of sugar in her teacup. "I hope you'll join us for Thanksgiving, Kelsey."

Her brother would be visiting his wife's family, and as was his habit, her father would spend the entire holiday working at the office. With Grampy at the Bar None, this year she'd figured she'd be alone. Martha Alice had invited her to the Breckenridge-Dolan family gathering, but this was the first Thanksgiving since Jack and Kate had married. She didn't want to intrude.

Incredibly touched, she folded her hands under her chin. "I'd love to join you and your family for Thanksgiving, Miss Dot. What can I bring?"

"Just yourself. It'll be the usual turkey and fixins' with pumpkin pie." Dorothy waved her blue-veined hand. "Everyone has their particular favorites."

"Isn't there something I could contribute?"

"No need to trouble yourself." Dorothy shrugged. "I'll take care of everything."

Dropping her gaze to the linen tablecloth, she nodded. "Oh. Okay. Thank you. It's very kind of you to include me in your family celebration." She traced her finger around the rim of the cup. Always the outsider looking in...

"On second thought."

She looked across the table at Clay's grandmother.

"I'd be nutty to refuse an offer to help with the cooking. So much to do." Dorothy lifted the teacup to her lips. "What dish means Thanksgiving to you?"

Kelsey perked. "Sweet potatoes."

"Sweet potatoes are a definite must." Dorothy smiled. "I do the traditional sweet potato casserole, but why don't we change it up this year? Do you have something in mind you'd like to bring?"

"I have the perfect recipe. Always a big hit. One of Grampy's favorites."

"That settles it, then." Dorothy took a sip of her tea. "I'm sure it will be wonderful. Howard won't be the only one glad to see you on Thanksgiving at the Bar None." She gave Kelsey a knowing look. "I'm thinking in particular of a certain cowboy."

Kelsey blushed. Of late, her thoughts were filled with a certain cowboy. The more time she spent with Clay, the less irritating she found him.

His relaxed outlook on life was growing on her. He made her laugh. With him, she felt like she could be herself. And she also felt safe. Since Granna's death, she'd wondered if she'd ever feel truly secure again.

Later, after dropping Dorothy at the ranch, she helped Martha Alice put together several items for her Thanksgiving dinner. Covering the cranberry chutney with plastic wrap, she told the older woman about Dorothy's invitation and her own contribution to the feast.

"I always loved that recipe." Martha Alice's eyes shone. "I'm happy you'll be with your grandfather over the holiday. Dorothy is a fantastic cook. Not fancy like Joan's gourmet cuisine but satisfying, good food."

Kelsey put the chutney in the refrigerator. "I've had my reservations about this wedding, but for the first time, I feel so hopeful." She let the refrigerator door swing shut behind her. "Like it's a chance for a brand-new start for us." She placed the apples needing to be peeled and quartered in a row on the countertop. "Like maybe there's a place for me."

"Oh, sweetie." Setting down the rolling pin, Martha Alice dusted the flour off her hands and came around the island.

She hugged Kelsey. "It has hurt my heart to see how you've struggled since Joan left us, but she would be so proud of the wonderful, generous young woman you've become. She'd want you to find someone to love and care for you, too."

Hands on her hips, Kelsey shook her head. "I'm sure I have no idea to whom you refer."

Martha Alice pursed her lips. "I'm equally sure you do."

"How about we get Grampy hitched before the Double Name Club starts on me?"

Martha Alice smirked. "I think that could be arranged."

Kelsey rolled her eyes. Once a matchmaker, always a matchmaker...

Early Wednesday morning, she stopped by the large grocery chain on the highway to purchase a few items she needed for Granna's signature Thanksgiving recipe. The store was filled with last-minute Thanksgiving shoppers. Holiday music played on the intercom.

Humming under her breath, she went through self-check-out to avoid the line. In the parking lot, the wind coming off the mountain gusted the brown leaves which had fallen to the ground around her car. She'd only just slid behind the wheel when her phone buzzed.

She clicked on. "Hi, Cowboy."

Clay's low, gravelly chuckle ignited butterflies inside her rib cage. "Hey yourself, Keltz."

She smiled into the phone.

"I hear you're coming to the ranch for Thanksgiving tomorrow."

Holding the phone to her ear with her shoulder, she pulled the seat belt taut and secured it. "I'm looking forward to coming to the ranch."

"I'm looking forward to seeing you," he rasped.

Good thing she was already sitting or else her knees might have buckled.

Kelsey heard the smile in his voice. She told him about Granna's recipe.

"Sweet potato rounds with ricotta cheese sounds to die for." His voice rumbled. "I happen to be an excellent food taster, if you're in the market for one."

Kelsey fished her keys out of her purse. "Granna's rule—taste testers have to help prepare the food."

"I'll have you know, Miss Summerfield, I am also an excellent sous-chef."

She inserted the key into the ignition. "Modest, too."

"One of my many admirable qualities, yes." He chuckled. "But I do know my way around the kitchen. Trained by the best. Thank you, Nana Dot. Are you headed to Marth'Alice's to put it together now?"

"Granna's recipe doesn't need to be prepared until the day of. By then, Marth'Alice's kitchen will be in full Thanksgiving mode. I'll go over to Grampy's condo tomorrow morning to make it so I won't be in her way."

"That's actually the real reason I called you. To see if I could pick you up so we could ride to the ranch together."

"I'd love to, but Grampy's condo would make it a farther commute for you."

"For me, it's a win-win. First dibs on the food and the added bonus of your company."

Her heart skipped a beat. He enjoyed being with her? "I don't want to be a bother."

"Stop doing that," he grunted.

Kelsey frowned into the phone. "Doing what?"

"You aren't a bother, Keltz. You're an amazing person. You're funny—"

"Funny like *ha ha*? Or funny *strange*?"

"Kelsey Summerfield," he groaned, "learn to take a compliment."

She bit back a sigh. Such a charmer. No wonder the women of Truelove went wild for him. "Thank you."

"Is that a *yes* then for sous-chef and escort?"

"A definite yes, but be prepared to work, McKendry."

"It's a date, then. I mean—"

A date… The butterflies in her chest did loop-de-loops. "What time should I arrive?"

"Is nine too early?"

Clay snorted. "By nine o'clock, darlin', this cowboy's done a half day's work and then some."

Her heart palpitated at the drawled out *darlin'*.

"See you tomorrow."

Her heart took flight. The holidays really were the most wonderful time of the year. She sang Christmas carols at the top of her lungs all the way to Truelove.

Thanksgiving morning in Truelove dawned bright, clear and cold. At the condo, she turned the holiday music on the stereo system up full blast and toed out of her calf boots. She set the oven to preheat. When the doorbell buzzed, she was doing the cha-cha-cha in the middle of the kitchen. She glanced at the clock on the wall: 8:59.

Kelsey loved a man who was early. *Whoa.* She stutter-stepped mid cha-cha-cha. Based on their short acquaintance, loved seemed a bit much. But what about *liked extremely*?

The doorbell buzzed again. She could definitely do *liked extremely* with Clay. Picking up the beat, she two-stepped her way to the entrance and flung open the door.

"Don't want to lose my place in the song," she shouted above the music. Grabbing his arm, she yanked him inside. "Dance with me, partner."

Never a dull moment with Kelsey Summerfield.

Keeping time in her bare feet, she threw him an outrageous grin. "We've got to practice for the wedding reception and show the old folks how it's done."

He had a feeling Mr. Howard and Nana Dot (who could do a swing dance with the best of them) would more likely show them how it was done. Setting an autumnal bouquet in a chair, he jumped into the beat with Kelsey.

Placing his hand softly on her shoulder, they joined their free hands and were off. Quick-quick, slow, slow. Quick-quick, slow, slow. They danced an imaginary line around the perimeter of the living-room furniture. Following his lead, she did a series of twirls. By the time the song ended, they were both laughing hard.

"Whew!" Gasping for breath, she fell onto the couch. "That was fun."

He fanned his face with his hat. Kelsey was fun.

She pointed her chin at the flowers lying abandoned on the armchair. "For me?"

He handed her the bouquet. "Happy Thanksgiving."

She unfolded from the sofa and buried her face in the blossoms. "They're beautiful. Thank you, Clay."

He got his first good look at her, and the bottom dropped out of his stomach. She was beautiful. Her sparkling blue eyes. The waves of dark cascading hair. Her feet were bare. Her toenails were painted to match her dress.

She smoothed a hand over the short lacy dress, which was the color of cranberries. "Do I look okay? Miss Dot said casual."

This was Kelsey's version of casual?

"You look great." She did. So great.

She smiled. "Thank you."

The next song playing on the condo's stereo system was slower. One of the old crooners from Nana Dot's generation. Something about home and Christmas.

Her eyes glistened. "I love that song," she whispered.

Clay swallowed past the lump in his throat. "Me, too."

Their gazes locked. For a moment, time tipped sideways. They shared a long look.

With a quivery sigh, she broke eye contact. "I'll put the flowers in a vase." On her way to the kitchen, she lowered the music volume. Slightly.

He stuffed his hands into his jean pockets. "Put me to work."

She set him in front of a cutting board to slice sweet potatoes into rounds one-quarter-inch thick. On the other side of the island, she whipped an herbed ricotta spread. "After you've sliced everything, massage the rounds with the avocado oil and seasoning."

"Let's keep Thanksgiving G-rated, Summerfield."

She rolled her eyes. "You are so ridiculous." She bustled over to show him how to prep the rounds. Soon, they transferred the sweet potato slices to a baking sheet and into the oven.

"While we wait to flip the rounds to bake on the other side, let's clean up." She handed him a dish towel. "I'll wash. You dry."

Another tune floated over the sound system. Hands in the soapy water, she warbled along to "O Christmas Tree." They stood shoulder to shoulder at the sink.

"I hadn't realized you're one of *those* people."

She stopped singing. "What people?"

He smirked. "The kind who insist on jump-starting Christmas. What ever happened to giving thanks on Thanksgiving?"

She flicked a soap bubble at him. "I happen to be very *thankful* for Christmas."

"I didn't know you liked to cook." He slung the towel over his shoulder. "You look at home in the kitchen."

She fluttered her lashes at him. "There's probably a lot you don't know about me, Cowboy."

His heart ratcheted. But oh, how he'd like to learn.

"Granna taught me everything I know. The kitchen was our special place together."

She checked the baking sheet in the oven. Following her instructions, he removed the pan and flipped the rounds to the other side. On a lower rack, she placed another tray of walnuts to roast. Finishing the dishes, she belted out "Hark! The Herald Angels Sing."

He grinned. "Didn't realize you were so *musical*, either."

She butted him with her hip. "Don't hate, Cowboy. Appreciate."

"I appreciate plenty. It's good to see you happy."

She leaned against the cool, smooth quartz of the countertop. "The sweet potato rounds were our thing at Thanksgiving. Making them today makes Granna feel close." She looked at him. "Thanks for adding a new memory to an old one."

"Thanks for inviting me."

Somehow the distance between them had lessened. If he leaned just a little, if she lifted her face just a tad… His heart jackhammered.

Her blue eyes widened. Moistening her bottom lip, she stared up at him. Did she want him to kiss her?

Clay put his hand to her waist. "Keltz…"

A vein in the tiny hollow of her throat pulsed. "Cowboy," she whispered. Standing on tiptoe, she lifted her face. Her lips parted. He lowered his head.

The oven timer dinged. They jolted apart. The moment broken, she rushed past him to check the sweet potatoes. Over the next few minutes, she barked out directions. She was good at giving orders.

Dotting the rounds with a dollop of herbed ricotta, he

swallowed a smile. Somehow, he didn't mind her bossiness as much as he would have a week ago. The rounds returned to the oven for a few minutes. Then they topped the rounds with walnuts and cranberries.

She drizzled honey over each one with a final flourish. "Ta-da!"

"Mmm…" His belly growled. "These look good. Feel free to cook for me anytime."

Slipping on a denim jacket, she laughed, not taking him seriously. "Such a flirt."

But he was serious. As a heart attack. He put his hand over his chest. The way his heart was feeling this morning, perhaps he ought to consult a cardiologist. Or maybe it was simply the Kelsey effect.

She transferred the rounds to a white platter.

"Hang on, Summerfield." He moved toward her. "Haven't I earned the right to a taste test?"

Kelsey's mouth quirked. "A taste test? That's what you want?"

For a second, his eyes drifted to her mouth before he caught her gaze. Their almost-kiss minutes earlier passed between them like a lightning bolt.

"Just one." She wagged her finger at him. "Save the rest for later."

"You talking about sweet potatoes?" He cocked his head. "Or something else?"

Smiling, she shook her head. "Whichever you prefer, Clayton."

He no longer minded as much when she used his given name.

"Now who's the flirt?" Laughing, he reached for the round. "Sweet potato first… It's called an appetizer for a reason. I'll save the other for later." He popped the warm round into his mouth.

"Promises, promises," she teased.

He chewed and swallowed. "Way to wow. Totally lives up to the hype."

She sashayed toward the couch. "So will a kiss."

He hooked his thumb in his belt loop. "Promises, promises."

She slipped into a pair of worn leather calf boots.

"Get a look at you, City Girl."

She did a slow twirl. "I'm embracing my inner cowgirl. What do you think?"

He sighed. "I think we better get on the road, or we're going to be late for Thanksgiving."

They entertained each other all the way to the ranch. Favorite Christmas carol. Favorite contemporary Christmas song. Fruitcake versus Christmas cake.

She sniffed. "You're a fruitcake."

"Takes one to know one." Veering off the secondary road, he drove under the crossbars of the Bar None. He pulled the truck up to the farmhouse. "Doesn't look like the parents are here yet."

"Your parents are coming?"

He cut the engine. "Dad wouldn't miss Turkey Day at Nana Dot's. They'll stay the entire weekend. Now you'll get to meet them before the wedding."

"Unlike my family."

He looked at her, but she avoided his eyes. Even though his dad had retired from ranch life to the beach, his family remained close. He'd given up trying to understand Kelsey's family dynamics.

Clay carried the sweet potato tray into the house. Nana Dot met them at the door. She offered him her cheek for a quick kiss.

Nana Dot took the platter. "Something smells scrumptious. Howard's resting in the living room."

Kelsey frowned. "Is he all right?"

"Not his usual chipper self." Nana Dot arched her eyebrow. "He's feeling out of sorts, but your lovely face will cheer him."

"Thanksgiving is his favorite holiday." Kelsey removed her jacket. "I hope he's not coming down with something."

Clay took off his coat. "Maybe he didn't sleep well."

His grandmother touched the lace on Kelsey's sleeve. "What a beautiful dress."

"Not too much?" Kelsey gave her a hesitant smile. "I considered jeans, but I thought if I paired the dress with the jacket and my boots…"

"It's perfect. You look a right picture." Nana Dot pushed her glasses up the bridge of her nose. "Doesn't she, Clay?"

"Yes, ma'am." He threw Kelsey a smile. "That she does."

It amazed him how she doubted herself sometimes. One thing he'd discovered about Kelsey over the last week— behind her super-confident competence lay a roiling mass of insecurities.

They followed his grandmother into the living room. In the recliner, Mr. Howard fiddled with the television remote.

Kelsey gave him a hug. "Happy Thanksgiving, Grampy."

Grunting, he patted her arm and returned to his investigation of the Thanksgiving Day football lineup. Clay cut his eyes at the older man. Not having a good day. Whatever ailed Mr. Howard, Nana Dot's cooking would soon set him right.

His stomach rumbled again. Cinnamon, cloves and other delicious aromas wafted through the house. Thinking of Nana Dot's pumpkin pie, his mouth watered.

Kelsey stepped forward. "How can I help you, Miss Dot?"

"I've got everything under control. Waiting on the turkey to come out of the oven. Clay's dad will carve it when he arrives. That's his Thanksgiving Day job. But I'd love your help to set the table."

"Counting Trudy, you're expecting seven for dinner?"

"*Dinner* sounds so fancy." Nana Dot gave her a side hug. "Around here on Thanksgiving, we do *lunch*. But actually, there'll be ten of us."

She looked at Clay. "Ten?" He shrugged.

Nana Dot patted Mr. Howard's shoulder. "An unexpected and delightful surprise."

Clay sat on the sofa. "Already did my Thanksgiving Day job."

Kelsey batted her lashes. "And what job would that be, Cowboy?"

He leaned his elbows on his knees. "I cracked the nuts for the pecan pie."

"You're a—"

"Go ahead and say it." He grinned. "You know you want to."

Sniffing, she clamped her lips shut.

Chuckling, Nana Dot set the platter on the coffee table. "Howard, Kelsey brought an appetizer. Would it be okay, Kelsey dear, if we don't wait for the others? I can't wait to try one."

"Of course." She smiled. "I hope you like it."

"I've been up since the crack of dawn, and I'm starving. So ingenious of you to think of bringing something to snack on until lunch." Nana Dot peeled off the aluminum. "If it tastes as good as it—"

"Sweet potato rounds!" With a roar, Grampy brought the recliner upright and thumped his feet down on the carpet. "What on earth possessed you to bring that here?"

Kelsey shrank back a step.

"What are you trying to prove?" He shook his finger

in her face. "Why must you always rub Dorothy's nose in it? Try to show her up."

"I-I wasn't." Kelsey's voice wobbled. "I didn't mean... It's just this is my favorite—your favorite..." She opened her hands. "I-I only wanted to share something special with..."

"Howard." Clay's grandmother put a hand on his shoulder. "Calm down. Kelsey didn't—"

"Did your father put you up to this?" Glaring at his granddaughter, Howard Summerfield turned toward Nana Dot. "She's trying to sabotage our happiness. I won't stand for it, I tell you. I won't."

Clay's jaw dropped. He'd never seen this side of Howard Summerfield. And after what Kelsey had let slip about her dad... Suddenly, he saw more than a passing resemblance between father and son.

His gaze swung to his grandmother. She appeared as shocked by the change in her usually congenial fiancé as Clay felt.

Nana Dot propped her hands on her bony hips. "You're overreacting, Howard. Kelsey wasn't—"

"Why must you spoil everything, Kelsey?" Howard fumed. "Why must you ruin Thanksgiving?"

"That's enough, Mr. Summerfield." Rising, Clay inserted himself between Kelsey and her grandfather. He clenched his hands at his side, trying hard not to disrespect the older gentleman. "I will not allow you to speak to Kelsey that way."

Her face stricken, Kelsey's eyes were huge. "I'm s-sorry." Tears cascaded down her cheeks.

Sobbing, she bolted out the door.

Chapter Ten

Blinded by tears and vaguely aware of raised voices, Kelsey stumbled out the door. Leaving chaos in her wake, she fled the farmhouse.

Moments later, she found herself pressed against a split-rail fence staring aimlessly at the evergreen forest beyond the pasture.

Since the shopping expedition, she and Dorothy had reached a good place with each other. Had she been trying to, as Grampy claimed, show up Miss Dot in comparison to Granna? Kelsey searched her heart for unconscious motivations. But she'd only meant to share something special to her. She had no idea Grampy would react that way. In all her twenty-six years, he'd never so much as raised his voice to her.

Kelsey choked back a sob. She might not be guilty of everything he accused her of, but perhaps the fault lay in not thinking it through. She'd not only angered her grandfather but hurt Dorothy, too. Thanksgiving, which had started out so right, was a disaster.

She was a disaster. She swiped away the tears on her cheeks. Fat lot of good crying had ever done her. It hadn't kept her mother from dying. It had only made her father run from her. It wouldn't fix this fiasco.

What was she going to do now? She couldn't return to the house. Maybe if she left, the McKendry holiday wouldn't be a complete debacle.

But having left her phone on the coffee table, she couldn't call for a rideshare or taxi. Not that Truelove had either service. Who could she call to pick her up at the road? Martha Alice's grandson, Jack, would come and get her. But it was Thanksgiving. She'd only wreck their plans.

She was so tired of being a burden. Of never belonging anywhere.

Her only recourse was to walk to Truelove. Not a great option, considering the heels on her boots. Truelove was miles away. Separated from the Bar None by several treacherous mountain roads. But at the moment, she didn't care what happened to her. She just wanted away.

"Kelsey."

She stiffened. Lost in misery, she hadn't heard Clay come out of the house. A wave of crimson flooded up her neck. He must think her the most horrible, insensitive person he'd ever met. Or the dumbest.

"Keltz?"

His little nickname stabbed like a knife in her heart. She squeezed her eyelids shut. "I-I'm okay." She flailed her arm behind her back. "Go inside with your family. I never meant—"

Clay caught hold of her arm. "What he said isn't true. That's not who you are. Would you look at me, darlin'?"

She shook her head. "I-I can't."

"It's cold out here, Keltz. The denim jacket is cute, but not enough for November in Truelove."

She let her shoulders rise and fall. "I'm okay with suffering for fashion."

"That's the spirit."

She heard the smile in his voice.

"But I'm not okay with you shaking like a leaf."

He opened his coat, and she found herself enfolded by his arms. The scents of hay, leather and something masculine, something totally him, engulfed her senses.

Clay was warm. And wonderful. And kind.

"Your grandfather had no right to say those things."

She was faintly amazed at the anger in his voice. No one had ever defended her before. Not any of the men in her life, anyway.

His arms tightened around her. "It wasn't true. I saw how you were this morning."

To be known and understood… To be accepted and cherished… A pinprick of tears stung her eyelids.

What would it be like to be loved by someone as fierce and loyal as Clay McKendry? Not that she'd ever know, of course. He'd proven himself a rare friend, but good men like him fell for sweet, uncomplicated women. Like the brunette who worked at the pharmacy.

Kelsey was a complete mess. The longer she stayed in his life, the bigger the risk she'd mess him up, too. But for just a moment… Just a few moments… She leaned her head against his chest and enjoyed the comfort of his arms.

Letting out a sigh, her breath fogged in the crisp, chill air. "I do ruin everything," she whispered.

Clay rested his stubbly chin on her head. "I don't believe that."

"I killed my mother. That's why my family is so messed up. Dad couldn't stand to look at me, and my brother Andrew couldn't stand to be near me."

"Kelsey," he growled, "you did not kill your mother."

"But I did." She turned in his arms. "After Andrew was born, my mother was diagnosed with an autoimmune disease. It made it harder for her to conceive, which is why there's a decade between Andrew and me. The doctors and Dad tried to dissuade her, but she was determined to have another child."

Clay lifted her chin with his finger. "She wanted you, Kelsey."

"Dad didn't." Her gaze caught his. "After I was born, she was never the same physically. It was the beginning of a decline that ended with her death when I was seven. Dad has never gotten over her loss. He buried himself in the company. Andrew made his own life. Granna and Grampy took me in to raise."

He pressed his forehead to hers. "No wonder losing your grandmother has been so hard for you. You must feel now you've lost your grandfather, too."

She pulled back a tad. "Today proves that I have."

He shook his head. "Something is going on with Mr. Howard, but I don't think it has anything to do with you. Come inside with me."

"I won't go where I'm not wanted."

He scowled. "I want you here."

"But Miss Dot—"

"Nana Dot knows your intentions were good."

She took a shuddery breath. "Could I borrow the keys to your truck? I can get it returned tonight."

"Please, Kelsey. Stay." He pulled her against him. "You haven't met my parents yet."

She rested her cheek against the soft flannel of his green-checked shirt. Through the fabric, she could feel the strong thumping of his heart. "Clay…" Of their own volition, her arms went around his waist.

"If you leave, I'm leaving, too." His voice roughened. "I won't have you spending Thanksgiving alone."

An impossible choice. Either she stayed where she

wasn't welcome, or she ruined the holiday for Clay. She'd spent a lifetime being unwanted, what was one more day if it meant salvaging Thanksgiving for him?

"Okay," she mumbled into his shirt. "I'll stay."

He drew back to examine her face. She immediately missed the warmth of him. "Really?"

She nodded.

"If he—" Jaw clenched, Clay jabbed his thumb at the house "—says anything else negative to you, I'll drive you to Asheville myself, and we'll make our own Thanksgiving."

She patted his chest. "My cowboy hero. It'll be fine."

He reached for her hand. She laced her fingers through his. Hand in hand, they strolled to the house. Dorothy met them on the porch.

"Oh, Miss Dot." Kelsey gulped. "I am so sorry."

Smelling of cinnamon spice, Dorothy's thin arms went around her. "You have nothing to be sorry about. Howard was in a mood. I told him in no uncertain terms he was out of line."

It did not escape Kelsey's attention Clay hadn't let go of her hand. Nor, apparently, his grandmother's, either. The older woman's questioning gaze cut between them. She patted Kelsey's shoulder and then laid a gentle hand upon Clay's cheek.

Dorothy turned to the door. "Howard and I had a long talk. I don't think he'll give you anymore grief."

Kelsey took a deep breath. Squaring her shoulders, she allowed Clay to tug her inside. A quick scan revealed the sweet potato tray still lying on the coffee table next to her phone. Her grandfather slumped in the recliner. "Kelsey, could we talk?"

Clay gripped her hand.

The gesture did not go unnoticed. Something brief as

to be almost nonexistent flickered in the older man's eyes. Grampy cleared his throat. "Alone."

Clay frowned.

She untangled her fingers from his. "It's okay."

"Are you sure?" he rasped.

She was anything but sure. However, hard situations were better faced straightaway. She'd learned that much the day of Granna's funeral. She nodded.

"Clay," Dorothy called from the kitchen, "would you take the turkey out of the oven for me?"

With a final look at her, Clay headed for the kitchen. Leaving Kelsey alone with her grandfather. Until today, a man she'd believed would never let her down. But that's what people did. They left, or they died. One way or the other, they always let her down.

Except Clay.

Her grandfather shuffled out of the recliner and to his feet. "I should've never said those things to you." His voice broke. "I'm sorry. Please forgive me."

"I'm the one who needs to ask forgiveness." She knotted her fingers together. "I didn't think. I—"

"You have nothing to apologize for." Grampy shook his head. "I'm a foolish old man."

She came around the coffee table. "No, you're not. I should never have—"

"I woke up thinking about your Granna this morning." His faded blue eyes moistened. "I miss her so much."

Kelsey touched his arm. "Me, too."

His Adam's apple bobbed. "I have so much more than I ever dreamed possible to be thankful for this year." His gaze darted toward the kitchen. "I felt guilty thinking about Joan when Dorothy and I are about to be married."

"Oh, Grampy."

He sighed. "With Joan's sweet potato rounds, which I

love, staring me in the face, the guilt just rose up. I took out my anger at myself on you." He squeezed her hand. "I hope I haven't ruined things between us. You've been the joy of my life."

A lump rose in her throat. "You haven't ruined anything. I love you, Grampy." She hugged him.

"I love you, too, honeybun."

"Could I give you a quick piece of advice?" She bit her lip. "Though, it's not like I have a ton of experience with marriage."

He chuckled. "Exactly none, but go ahead. Say what you've got to say."

"I only wanted to remind you that you and Granna were married for nearly sixty years. You spent so many Thanksgivings together. Don't you think it's normal to miss someone you shared a lifetime with? And still perfectly okay to look forward to a new beginning with someone else?"

He gave her a faint smile. "Dorothy said the same thing."

Kelsey heaved a sigh of relief. "I'm glad you talked it over with her."

"Polka Dot and I are on track again. No worries. I plan to offer an apology to Clay, too." He reached for a sweet potato round and took a bite. "Delicious. Just like your Granna's."

Yet despite his assurances, a small worry niggled at her. Was Grampy getting cold feet? Granna had only been dead a year. Was he truly ready to get married again? In rushing forward with the wedding, was he glossing over his doubts?

She wanted what was best for him and Miss Dot. The prospect of keeping her grandfather to herself no longer held the allure it might have several weeks ago. She'd seen how happy Dorothy made him.

Kelsey had only just joined Clay and his grandmother

in the kitchen when his parents arrived. She stayed where she was, setting the silverware around the dining-room table. Clay went to greet his parents.

Ushering her son and daughter-in-law into the house, Dorothy introduced them to Grampy. Kelsey peeked around the half-wall partition. From the way he fiddled with the buttons on the charcoal sweater vest, she could tell he was nervous. Like her, he'd overdressed for a McKendry Thanksgiving.

He'd worn his usual version of dressed-down casual—a starched white shirt and pressed gray wool pants straight from the dry cleaners. And the crowning touch? To Grampy's mind, the penultimate token to casualness, a sweater vest.

"Kelsey, stop for a minute." Arms folded and booted ankles crossed, Clay leaned against the wall. "Come meet my parents."

Heart inexplicably pounding, she bit the inside of her cheek. Why did this feel like such a huge deal? She felt a surge of sympathy for Grampy.

"Keltz." He held out his hand. "I promise they're much nicer than me."

"A low bar there, Cowboy."

"You'll like my mother." He threw her a crooked grin, setting her knees aquiver. "Mom will love you for your efforts to keep me humble."

"A thankless job, but somebody's gotta do it."

They headed for the living room. She'd never known such an astonishing amount of comfort could be communicated through the simple touch of his hand against the small of her back. He introduced her to his parents.

Clay had inherited his height from his father, Gary. Perhaps one day also his father's slightly receding hairline? She swallowed her smile. Either way, Clay McKendry would still possess the power to wow. Her, at least.

Grampy shoved the platter of sweet potato rounds at Clay's father. "Try these. A Summerfield Thanksgiving tradition. Kelsey made them."

"Don't mind if I do." Gary helped himself. "Yum. Great job, Kelsey."

Smiling, Clay's eyes caught hers. She nudged him with her shoulder. "You're right. They are nicer than you," she rasped.

His mother hooted. Kelsey went scarlet. Her and her big—

Susan McKendry slipped her arm around Kelsey. "I think we're going to be friends. Has my son told you about the time in high school when he—"

"Not fair to gang up, Mom."

Steering Kelsey toward the kitchen, his mother fluttered her hand at him. "Keep your dad and Mr. Howard company, baby boy. Kelsey and I are going to have a chat."

"Don't embarrass me, Mom."

Susan winked at Kelsey. He'd gotten his sense of humor from his mother. Kelsey threw him a marginally wicked smile. Kind of fun to turn the tables on him. He was right, although she'd never tell him so. She liked his down-to-earth parents.

A few minutes later, his Aunt Trudy arrived with a green bean casserole. She added another layer of good-natured fun to the gathering. Dorothy called Gary to his turkey-carving duties. Kelsey finished setting the table. Clay had a hard time standing idle. Dorothy put him in charge of making sure the biscuits didn't burn. As Susan removed the biscuits from the oven, a flurry of knocks sounded at the front door.

"Let Kelsey answer the door!" Dorothy hollered.

She jerked. Susan nearly dropped the pan of biscuits.

"Me?" Kelsey pointed to herself. "Shouldn't Clay or—"

"I'll put the food on the table." Dorothy shooed her toward the living room. "You welcome the rest of our guests."

Who is it? she mouthed at Clay.

Eyebrows raised, he shrugged.

She passed Grampy, engrossed in the Thanksgiving Day parade on television. He was of the generation that it would never occur to him to help in the kitchen. He brought home the bacon. It had been up to Granna to fry it up in the pan. Kelsey's grandmother had waited on him hand and foot. For the sake of future marital harmony, she prayed Miss Dot was of like mind.

Kelsey yanked open the door. Whatever she believed she might find on the doorstep, she'd never in a million years have guessed it would be her brother and his family.

Five-year-old Eloise threw her arms around her. "Aunt Kelsey!"

"Andrew? Nicola?" Eloise's exuberance almost knocked her off her feet. She caught hold of the doorframe. "What are you doing here?"

Eloise let go of her. "We're here to eat turkey and see the horses."

"And?" Kelsey's London-born sister-in-law prompted.

Eloise's brow creased. "Oh, yeah." Her face lit. "Meet Grampy's new family."

Kelsey glanced over her shoulder to find the McKendrys standing in the foyer behind her. "These are your surprise guests, Miss Dot?"

Dorothy came forward. "I can't tell you how pleased I am to finally meet Howard's grandson." Propping her hands on her knees, she bent toward Kelsey's niece. "You must be Eloise. I've heard so much about you."

Grampy gave Andrew a big hug and performed the introductions.

Kelsey looked at her brother. "Aren't you supposed to be in Tucson with Nicola's family?"

"Nicola's parents came down with the flu." With the tip of his finger, Andrew pushed his black framed glasses higher on the bridge of his nose. "We thought it would be nice to spend Thanksgiving in North Carolina for a change."

His wife, tall and elegant, gave Kelsey a hug. "Andrew called Dorothy. And we sort of invited ourselves."

Dorothy waved her hand. "You did nothing of the kind. I'm so pleased we can be together on Thanksgiving Day."

Eloise begged to see the horses, but Clay promised her a tour after lunch. Gary sat at the head of the table. Dorothy sat at the other end with Grampy on one side. The rest of them filled in the other seats. Eloise insisted on sitting beside Kelsey, warming her heart. Clay pulled the chair next to Kelsey.

Gary said a short grace, and everyone dug in. Platters of turkey were passed around. Trays of ham. The gravy boat. There was a great deal of laughter and joy. Clay was incredibly good with Eloise. Who knew he'd be such a natural with kids? Like females of all ages, it didn't take her niece long to succumb to his effortless charm.

She couldn't stop gazing in wonder around the table. How had this happened? When was the last time her family had gathered for a happy occasion?

He touched her hand under the table. "You okay?" His breath fluttered a stray tendril of hair against her neck.

She was better than okay. Amidst the clatter of cutlery and animated chatter, this was what a real family was supposed to be like. Something, she realized with an acute clarity, she wanted very much for herself. She cut her eyes at Clay.

Kelsey wasn't above admitting to a growing fondness for pickup trucks.

"Why are you smiling?"

"No reason." She smiled again. "Just happy."

He squeezed her hand under the table. "I'm glad." He caught her gaze and held it.

Gary cleared his throat. "Earth to Clay. Kelsey? Would one of you pass the butter?"

Looking away, she discovered all eyes glued on them. She blushed. How long had Clay's father been trying to get their attention? Grampy hid a grin behind his napkin. Dorothy exchanged a meaningful look with Nicola.

Giving her a lopsided grin that made her toes curl in her boots, Clay passed the butter dish. "Sure, Dad."

The earlier hope she'd tried to communicate with Martha Alice returned.

She wasn't losing Grampy. She was gaining a new family. Her heart ratcheted a notch. Maybe a cowboy, too.

Chapter Eleven

After lunch, his parents and Aunt Trudy insisted on cleaning up the dishes. They sent Nana Dot into the living room to keep Mr. Howard company. Clay gave the Summerfields the Bar None grand tour. It was fun seeing the ranch through Eloise's contagious excitement.

He turned three of the horses into the paddock. In her black patent leather shoes, Eloise climbed onto the fence rail and hung over the gate. Kelsey and Nicola stood on each side to make sure she didn't pitch headfirst into the corral.

Comparing ranch life with the corporate life, Clay and Kelsey's brother ambled along the fence line. Kelsey's family was both less and more than he'd expected. Obviously, Summerfield casual attire standards were very different from McKendrys.

Wearing a hunter green sweater with leather elbow patches and tassel-fringed loafers that probably cost as much as a month's worth of gasoline for the tractor, Andrew was the epitome of success. Andrew's wife, glamorous Nicola, with her fancy British accent added to the image of sophistication. But like Kelsey, Andrew and his family were genuine, kind and unpretentious.

"I admire what concerned citizens have done to revitalize Truelove's downtown." Andrew pushed his slightly hipster, dark-framed eyeglasses farther along his nose. "Grampy told me about it. Too many of the small Appalachian towns are dying."

Clay scuffed his boot in the dirt. "There aren't many good-paying jobs. People leave for the city. There's also the lack of access to health care and broadband in the rural areas."

Andrew nodded. "I'd like to see other communities flourish again like Truelove."

"I wouldn't exactly call Truelove flourishing, not yet, but there's a whole lot more hope out there than you would've found even five years ago.

"That's what excites me." Andrew's eyes gleamed. "Being part of the solution."

Clay cocked his head. "How so?"

"The Summerfields have done a lot to develop western North Carolina. I'd like to add an additional legacy to the company Grampy started—by providing resources and opportunities to revitalize small towns in the region."

"Is your father on board with this project?"

Andrew frowned. "I'm working on him. It's a passion of mine and Grampy's. It's time the Summerfields gave back to the people and the state who've given us so much." He jutted his jaw. "If I have to, I'm prepared to start my own nonprofit to make it happen."

"You'd leave Summerfield, Inc.?"

"Nicola would, too." Andrew crossed his arms. "For the sake of my relationship with Dad, I hope it won't come to that."

Clay couldn't ignore this opportunity to make her brother aware of the deep pain Kelsey carried. "This is absolutely none of my business, but did you know Kelsey blames herself for your mother's death? Do you have any idea how isolated and alone she's felt since your grandmother died last year?" He made an effort to not raise his voice, but every time he recalled Kelsey's forlorn face that morning, he wanted to rip somebody apart for hurting her.

Andrew shook his head. "I've never blamed her for what happened."

Clay folded his arms. "And your father?"

Andrew ran his hand over his dark hair. "My mother's death made him a bitter man. Unfortunately, Kelsey took the brunt of his inability to face his loss. I was seventeen when Mom died." His eyes shone with remembered pain. "There was a huge age gap between us, but that's no excuse. I was dealing with my own grief, but I should've been there for her." He blinked rapidly. "And caught up with the business and family, I've done it to her again after Granna died, haven't I?" He gulped. "I'm sorry."

"You should talk to Kelsey."

Andrew gave him a slight smile. "I still remember the day Mom brought her home from the hospital. I was excited. She was such a little thing."

"Still is," Clay grunted.

"I've always been so happy she became part of our family."

"You should tell her that. It would mean a lot."

"I will."

They'd looped around to the ladies. Kelsey had found a length of rope with which she endeavored to lasso a fence post, much to Eloise's delight.

She waved. "Look at me."

"Harnessing that inner cowgirl?" Clay called.

She grinned at him. "Don't you know it."

Andrew laughed. "My sister is something, isn't she?"

She was something, all right.

Kelsey handed him the rope. "Show us what you got, Cowboy."

He threw the lasso, hitting the target the first time.

Eloise applauded.

Kelsey smiled. "Show-off."

He reeled in the rope. "Practice makes perfect."

She climbed onto the fence beside her niece. "Hear the noise the cows are making, Eloise?"

"I hear them, Aunt Kelsey." Eloise held onto the top rail. "Why?"

"The noise they're making, dear niece..." Kelsey dropped her voice, and Eloise leaned closer "...is what we call *lowing*, like in the Christmas carol."

Eloise's forehead scrunched. Andrew chuckled.

Clay shoved his hands in his pockets. "Come again?"

"'Away in a Manger'!" Eloise shrieked. "'The cattle are lowing'," she sang.

"'—the baby awakes'..." Kelsey warbled.

Holding onto the top-most rail, they sang the rest of the carol to the cows.

Nicola returned to the house, but Eloise wanted to help feed the herd.

Clay gave her fancy dress and patent leather shoes a skeptical look.

Andrew shrugged. "She's only little once. Let her enjoy herself." Opting to take a stroll around the ranch, he asked Kelsey to walk with him. Surprised but pleased, Kelsey joined him.

With the old ranch truck already loaded with hay and a protein supplement, Clay and Eloise headed out to deliver the feed. The ruts in the frozen ground jostled Eloise, perched beside him on the seat inside the truck cab.

"I don't see any cows, Clay. Will they know where to find us?"

"Look over there." He pointed over the rise to a cluster of cattle making their way toward them. "Just like kids and ice cream trucks, the cows hear this old contraption and come to us."

Eloise appeared to be having the time of her life, patent leather shoes and all. These Summerfield women. Apparently, it didn't take much to delight them.

On the return trek to the barn, he spotted Andrew and Kelsey on the porch. Her eyes looked puffy and red-rimmed. Clay stiffened. But then Andrew hugged her hard. Her brother's eyes didn't look too dry, either.

Later inside the farmhouse, Nana put her arm around Eloise. "While I've got such good helpers here, let's decorate the Christmas tree."

Kelsey cut her eyes around the living room. "What Christmas tree?"

"The one I bought from Luke Morgan's Christmas tree farm and hauled over here last night." Clay smirked. "My other big Thanksgiving job. And here you thought I was only good for cracking nuts."

"You are a nut, Clay," Eloise piped up.

"Eloise!" Nicola scolded.

"Truth," his mother declared.

Kelsey elbowed him. "Out of the mouths of babes."

Everyone laughed, including him.

"Yep." He elbowed Kelsey back. "When it comes to cowboy-bashing, the Summerfields are fitting right in."

She smiled. "Show me where to find the ornament boxes, Gingersnaps."

He opted to ignore the aspersion regarding his hair, choosing instead to believe she meant it as an endearment. Eloise wanted to go with them so he led them to the attic where the boxes were stacked under the eaves. One by one, he toted them to the second floor. Eloise dogged his every step, chatting about her favorite nuts—Clay and cashews.

Kelsey laughed so hard she had tears in her eyes.

The silvery star tree-topper clutched in her arms, Eloise scampered downstairs.

He shook his head. "Why does it come as no surprise to me your niece has a favorite nut, too?"

"Sorry to be such a bad influence." She didn't look sorry at all.

He heaved a mock sigh. "Don't I know it."

She fluttered her lashes. "Does that mean you're finding me irresistible?"

"That's one word for it."

Grabbing a box of red ribbons, she followed Eloise downstairs.

Clay and Andrew set the tree up in the living room. His parents strung the lights. Kelsey, Eloise and Nicola placed the ornaments on the evergreen boughs. Sipping coffee, Nana and Mr. Howard sat on the sofa, enjoying the Christmas activity. Like a vivacious Christmas butterfly, Kelsey flitted around, having as much fun as her niece. He enjoyed watching them together. She would make a great mother one day.

He blinked away a vision of a little boy or girl running around the barnyard in cowboy boots with not-red hair and cornflower-blue eyes.

Andrew and Nicola offered to take Mr. Howard to the condo to gather more clothes for his extended stay at the ranch. Clay and Andrew tucked him into the back seat of the SUV next to Eloise.

Howard rolled down the window. "I'll be back before you can miss me."

Nana gave him a quick peck on the forehead. "I already miss you."

"Thanks for the heads-up about my little sister." An-drew's gaze drifted to Kelsey hugging Nicola goodbye. "We had a good talk."

He and Andrew shook hands. "I'm glad." There was a lightness to Kelsey that hadn't been there before.

Nicola hugged his grandmother. "Thank you for what has been the most wonderful of Thanksgivings, Miss Dot."

Kelsey came around the car toward her brother. "Grampy's pain is better, and he'll enjoy the drive, but—"

"I'll pack what he needs, and he can stay in the car with Eloise." Andrew smiled. "Stop worrying. We'll take care of him and bring him back to the ranch later tonight."

"Next time we see you, Aunt Kelsey," Eloise called from the back seat, "I'm going to be a flower girl."

Kelsey grinned. "The best flower girl ever."

She and Andrew hugged. Her brother got behind the wheel.

Nana waved them off. "The outing will be good for Howard." She, Clay and Kelsey watched them drive away. "Cooped up in the house the last few weeks, he's getting stir-crazy."

Kelsey's grandfather had caught him alone earlier and offered his apologies for his overreaction. But the display of emotion had set Clay thinking. It ought to have set Nana Dot thinking, too.

They walked into the house.

"It's been so wonderful being with everyone today." Kelsey hugged Nana Dot. "But I should probably return to Marth'Alice's. Clay?"

"Let me get my hat."

His grandmother fluttered her hand. "No need to rush away. Stay for leftovers."

"I appreciate the invitation, but I'm sure you could use some downtime." Kelsey grabbed her purse and phone.

"Good news, Clay. You get Friday off. But Saturday afternoon, it's back to wedding planning."

He made a growling noise.

"You'll enjoy Saturday's excursion." She batted her eyes at him. "We're taking Grampy and Miss Dot to meet Maddie Lovett, the baker you recommended, to discuss wedding-cake options."

He smiled. She'd listened to him, valued his opinion and taken his suggestion. Her gesture of goodwill did not go unappreciated. "Will this involve taste testing?"

Kelsey slung her purse strap over her shoulder. "It does. Flavors, fillings and icing."

He stuck his thumbs in the belt loops of his jeans. "I can handle cake."

"I figured as much." She smirked. "Totally in your wheelhouse."

They smiled at each other.

"It'll be fun." She nodded. "Something to look forward to."

He liked to give Kelsey a hard time about wedding planning, but any time spent with her was something he looked forward to.

"I think I'll have a lie-down before supper." Nana Dot said her goodbyes. "See you Saturday."

On the ride to Truelove, Kelsey held the flowers he'd given her in her lap for safekeeping. She'd brought them to the ranch with her. The temperature had dropped throughout the day. The forecast called for an extended cold period over the next few weeks with the possibility of snow.

He glanced out the window at the distant mountain horizon. Like icing on a cake, the higher elevations already held a layer of snow. "You may get your wish for a wintry wedding."

"Woo-hoo!" She bounced in the seat. "What are you most thankful for, Clay?"

His lips quirked at the sudden change in topic. "Family. The ranch. Food. A good horse. What about you?"

"Family. The wedding. Turkey. A great Black Friday sale."

He rolled his eyes. Smiling, she snuggled against his side.

"There is one more thing I'm thankful for this year."

She looked at him. "What's that?"

"You."

Her face softened. "That may be the nicest thing anyone has ever said to me. Thank you, Clay." She lay her cheek against the sleeve of his coat. "Right back at you."

Clay's heart kicked up a notch. She wasn't like anyone he'd ever known. He had trouble recalling why he'd been so uptight about spending time with her. Whatever it was with her felt good and right and…inevitable?

The notion didn't fill him with the terror such an idea would have inspired within him a few weeks ago.

At Martha Alice's, he steered into the empty driveway. "Looks like the Dolans have gone home." He reached for the key in the ignition.

"No need to walk me to the door." Kelsey lay her hand atop his, igniting sparks along his nerve endings. "Whoops. Must be a lot of static electricity in the air today."

"Electricity." For real. "My mother would have my head if I didn't walk a lady to the door."

Her mouth twitched. "All right, then. In the interests of keeping your head attached to your shoulders."

Clay held the flowers while she scooted out. On the porch, he handed the bouquet to her.

"Thank you for sharing your family with me." Her voice went a shade husky. "I'll see you Saturday at the Jar for the taste testing."

Staring at her lips, his brow creased. Taste testing? Oh. Yeah. Cake. Right.

Rising on her tiptoes, she brushed her mouth across his cheek. "Until then."

His heart thudded. Waggling her fingers at him, she slipped inside the house.

Returning to the ranch, the memory of her lips lingered. His hand touched the spot on his cheek. It was no longer a matter of if but when he kissed her.

Something to look forward to, indeed.

At the Bar None, he hummed a Christmas song under his breath. Hearing noises from the barn, he found Aunt Trudy and his parents putting final touches on the Mason Jar Café float for Saturday's Christmas parade.

His dad tacked a length of gold metallic float sheeting to the sides of the trailer. "I like that girl, son."

Deliberately misunderstanding him, Clay grabbed a hammer. "Eloise is very sweet."

His mom threw a tissue-paper snowball at him. He ducked. "Your father means Kelsey. I like her, too. And I love where that relationship seems to be heading."

"We're just friends."

"You keep telling yourself that, nephew." Hand on her hip, his Aunt Trudy cackled. "Whatever helps you sleep at night."

Grinning, he left them to it and took the opportunity to check on his grandmother, napping in her room.

Careful of creaking boards in the old farmhouse, he peeked around the doorframe. Her head resting on the pillow, his grandmother lay stretched out on top of the bedspread with her eyes closed. A handmade blue-and-white crocheted afghan covered her.

Easing away, he decided not to disturb her. He'd talk to her later.

"Might as well come in, Clay."

"I'm sorry, Nana. I didn't mean to wake you."

Nana Dot reached for her glasses on the nightstand. "I wasn't asleep. Just pondering the day."

Was this the opening he'd been hoping for? He felt it his duty to discuss his concerns, but he didn't want to offend her or create distance between them. "About that…"

Nana sat up. "You want to talk about what happened with Howard this morning."

"Don't you think we should?" Clay leaned against the door. "I'm really trying not to butt into your business."

"Then, don't."

At her sharp words, he tensed. Easy-going Nana Dot had never used that tone with him before. He experienced more than a grudging sympathy for how Kelsey must've felt earlier.

"Howard apologized to you and explained what led to his outburst."

Recalling Kelsey's complete devastation, he stiffened. "An explanation doesn't excuse what he said to her."

"No, it does not. But Howard and I talked through the situation."

"You were satisfied with his explanation?"

"I am." She pursed her lips. "Howard was having an uncharacteristically bad day. We all have them." She leveled a look at him. "Including you."

Removing his hands from his pockets, he took a step into the room. "How uncharacteristic was it, though? How well do you—do any of us—know Howard Summerfield? No one would blame you for having second thoughts. For putting the brakes on your upcoming—"

"I am not a child, Clayton."

His gut tanked. This was not going well.

"I know everything I need to know about my fiancé."

Clay raked his hand over his head. "I'm not trying to upset you, Nana, but marriage is a serious commitment."

She laughed out right. "That's rich advice coming from Mr. Don't Fence Me In. What Howard was feeling this morning is only natural. He's new to bereavement."

"Which is exactly my point, Nana. His wife has only been dead a year."

Spots of color dotted her cheeks. "Howard and I are getting married next weekend. I suggest you deal with your own commitment issues before you go handing out unsolicited and unwelcome advice."

Clay's chest heaved. "I'm sorry, Nana. It was not my intention to upset you."

She flung the coverlet aside. "Well, you have. I'm stung you have such little faith in my judgment." She shook her bony finger. "I'm not senile yet, young man." She fumbled for her shoes on the floor beside the bed.

Getting down on one knee, he scooted them to within her reach. "I love you, Nana. You deserve only the best."

Lips pressed tight, she slipped on her shoes. "For me, Howard Summerfield is the best."

What a disastrous end to a day that had begun with such promise when he'd picked up Kelsey this morning.

"Please don't be angry with me," he rasped. "I'm only trying to look out for your best interests."

She glowered. "I'm perfectly capable of looking out for my own best interests."

"Yes, ma'am."

Nana glared at him another second. "Are you aware it's nearly impossible to stay angry at a contrite cowboy on one knee with good manners?" She laid a cool, brown-spotted hand gently against his cheek.

Something coiled inside him loosened.

"No, ma'am, I was not aware of that fact. But I promise

to keep that in mind next time I make somebody mad." He offered his arm as she rose from the bed.

"'Course, I won't guarantee it'll work on every woman." She arched her brow. "Kelsey Summerfield is far more sophisticated than me. She might just laugh in your face."

"I daresay you're probably right."

"Best not tick her off, then."

"I'll try to remember that, Nana."

"See that you do." Straightening, she smoothed her slacks. "We good?"

"Yes, ma'am." He hugged her. "We're good."

Patting his shoulder, she stepped away from him. "Your father will be wanting a turkey sandwich."

He walked her downstairs. But he couldn't help reflecting it wasn't characteristic of mild-mannered Nana Dot to be so defensive. Unless deep down, she harbored her own doubts about her upcoming wedding to Howard.

A sharp sense of foreboding needled him.

It was like seeing a car stalled on the railroad tracks. A train of reckoning was coming. And he was helpless to prevent the collision.

Chapter Twelve

Unlike every other Friday after Thanksgiving in her living memory, Kelsey did not spend the day shopping. With Clay and his family busy at the ranch, she decided to put together a business proposal for creating her event planning business—just for fun. With her relationship on the upswing with her father, maybe she could get him to look it over and, based on his experience running a company, offer her a few suggestions.

Not a person who thrived on silence, she took her laptop and a calculator to a corner booth at the Jar. At the register, Trudy sent her a little wave, but she and the waitresses were rushed off their feet with the breakfast crowd. Kelsey ordered a chai latte and got to work. Only when the bell above the entrance jangled with increasing frequency did she pull her head out of her notes. Blinking, she scanned the diner, filled to capacity since she'd last lifted her gaze. With a glance at the clock on the wall over the bulletin board, she realized she'd worked through breakfast and into lunch.

The petite blonde café owner, Kara MacKenzie, approached the booth.

Hastily, Kelsey gathered her materials. "I am so sorry to have taken your booth out of circulation all morning."

Smiling, Kara shrugged. "It was fine. What are you working on so intently?"

It occurred to her that the chef was a successful entrepreneur in her own right.

"I'd love your input on a plan I'm putting together for a local business start-up I'm contemplating. Perhaps I could discuss it with you when you're free."

"I'm free now." Kara sat down on the opposite bench. "Since Trudy has taken over the day-to-day management, I mainly come by in the mornings to get the lunch special going." She threw Kelsey a bittersweet smile. "Now that I've also trained Leo, our former short-order cook, in the fine art of French country cuisine, he really doesn't need me as much, either. Somehow I've worked myself out of a job."

Kelsey laughed.

"I'd like to hear about this project of yours. I'm about anything that brings more business to Truelove."

Turning the laptop around, she outlined her scheme to open an event venue. She also detailed her experience in planning various corporate events for her father's company over the last four years. "It's just an idea. Not sure I could ever come up with the capital to make it happen."

"You'll need investors. Are you thinking of building a venue or using an already existing site?"

Kelsey sighed. "Biggest line on my proposed budget is acquiring a property. Specific location yet to be determined. Although, if I had plenty of investors and dreams came true…"

"Why don't you think dreams can come true?" Kara tilted her head. "What are you dreaming of?"

An image of a certain cowboy flitted through her brain. Her cheeks warmed. No way was she admitting to that impossible dream. Dreaming of Birchfield seemed tame by comparison.

She extended her phone across the table. "Have you ever been to the top of Laurel Mountain Road?"

Kara scrolled through the photos she'd snapped of the house and grounds. "I had no idea something like this existed on the outskirts of Truelove. Like you, I'm not from around here." She glanced from the phone to Kelsey. "Tell me what you're thinking of doing here."

"Birchfield could host parties for every occasion. But primarily, we'd offer all-inclusive packages with top-notch accommodations for wedding parties. This would be a bride's one-stop shop for all things surrounding her special day."

"Food, too?" Kara scanned the photos again. "The kitchen would need updating with commercial equipment."

Kelsey nodded. "I'd offer a small preferred-vendor list for everything else, but we'd have an in-house chef. I'd want Birchfield to be renowned for its fine-dining experience."

"When you dream, girl, you dream big." Kara handed the phone back to her. "But first let's talk about the really crucial issue."

Kelsey tilted her head. "What's that?"

"Why don't you believe dreams can come true?" Kara's eyes, the color of blueberries, narrowed. "My life is living proof they can and do."

Over another round of coffee, Kara shared her story. As a child, she'd been homeless and orphaned until adopted by a legendary queen of North Carolina barbecue fame. Her mother, Glorieta Ferguson, was the successful owner of a chain of Southern down-home cooking establishments.

Kara sipped from her coffee mug. "Now I have the most wonderful husband in the world. My son, Maddox, who is my very heart. And this dear little café." Her gaze misted. "Dreams do come true."

In spite of her humble beginnings, Kara's other passion besides creating spectacular food was giving a hand up, not a handout, to those around her. Paying it forward, Kara gave back to the surrounding community. The food bank and county homeless shelter were weekly recipients of the Jar's bounty. She'd also established a scholarship to send local youth interested in the culinary arts to the program from which Kara had graduated in Charlotte.

That generosity of spirit, Kelsey realized, was the crux of the difference between someone like Kara and her own family. Her dad was only interested in their bottom-line profit for the company. Was she any better than her father, though?

Far too often, she'd focused on her own self-interest with no thought for the larger picture. She mulled over how she might incorporate the same model of helping others into any future business of her own.

Kara insisted she join her for lunch. Over the chef's signature Madame Croquette sandwiches, they talked and laughed. Kara was especially interested in the innovative foodie scene in Asheville that Kelsey had firsthand knowledge about.

"I've been toying with the idea of concentrating my skills once again on more haute cuisine." The chef laid her hands flat on the table. "I have some capital set aside. I'd be extremely interested in becoming involved in a partnership like the one you're proposing for your event venue." She shrugged. "If you'd be interested in working with me."

Kelsey's breath caught. "I'd love to work with you, Kara." Securing a chef with her skills and business savvy would go a long way toward making her dream a reality. "It's early days yet, though. It may not ever come to anything."

"It will." Kara patted her hand. "You don't give yourself enough credit. You remind me of my mother, Glorieta. You've got everything you need to succeed."

"Except money."

"The barbecue queen started her culinary empire as a single mom with practically nothing going for her but for a belief in herself." Kara squeezed her hand. "It'll happen. She's taught me a gut instinct for this kind of thing."

Kelsey smiled. "With you in the kitchen, the sky's the limit. Care to shake on it?"

The petite chef grinned. "Sure thing, partner."

Of course right now, they were partners of exactly nothing. But with Kara's faith in her, she suddenly felt her dream might not be so impossible after all.

They talked some more, but finally Kara excused herself to discuss tomorrow's menu with Leo. Kelsey knew she'd found a friend and potential business partner in the creative Mason Jar owner.

She spent the rest of the day finalizing her business proposal, her plan now also including Kara MacKenzie. Surely her dad couldn't help but be impressed by the chef's extensive credentials. That night, she wrote a short email to her father, attaching the document and asking for his opinion. Before she lost her nerve, she quickly hit Send.

Not long after, Clay texted to see if she wanted to go to the Truelove Christmas parade on Saturday. The next morning, he came by for her. Leaving his truck at Martha Alice's, they walked the few blocks over to Truelove's downtown.

From the mounted loudspeakers at the edge of the town square, strains of "Winter Wonderland" provided a festive note. Friends called out greetings to each other. Pretty much what seemed the entire population of Truelove, North Carolina, had turned out for the annual parade. And also for the free hot apple cider, courtesy of the Mason Jar.

She was struck by Kara's giving heart. Not too shabby

a business move, either, to get people in the café to order something more. After the parade, Clay spotted Sam and Lila, waiting in line with their little girl to see Santa.

Clay made a sweeping gesture. "Small-town charm at its finest." He took her arm. "Let's go see Santa on the square."

"Going to hand him your wish list, Clayton?" she teased.

"This Christmas looks like all my wishes are already coming true." He winked. She blushed. "But seeing the matchmakers in elf costumes is worth the wait."

"GeorgeAnne Allen is in an elf costume?"

"She's surprisingly good with the kids." He grinned at Kelsey. "But it boggles the mind, doesn't it? Seeing is believing."

It was indeed worth the wait.

Emma Cate looked adorable sitting in Santa's lap in the square.

GeorgeAnne arched a look at her. "You can wipe that smirk off your face, missy. Next year, you might just find yourself taking a turn as Santa's helper. You'd prove a very believable elf."

Clay laughed.

Her denim-blue eyes crinkling, ErmaJean handed him a green-striped candy cane. "Just so you know, after this wedding we're coming for you next, McKendry."

Clay's laughter turned into a sudden fit of coughing.

Kelsey pounded him on the back. "Small-town charm at its finest, Cowboy."

Emma Cate giggled.

At the firehouse, Clay introduced her to some of his friends. Lila made sure she met other young women her age. Everywhere, children played and skipped and bounced with the joy that was Christmas.

Kelsey had a sudden vision of herself attending many Truelove Christmas parades in the future. Strolling the square on the arm of a handsome certain somebody. Maybe with a little boy or a little girl. In cowboy boots?

She darted her gaze at Clay. He and Sam were taking turns pushing Emma Cate on the swings at the school playground. As if feeling her eyes on him, breaking off mid-sentence, Clay lifted his head and smiled at her.

Lila nudged Kelsey. "He likes you, you know."

Her cheeks warmed. "He—we—haven't even kissed."

Lila smiled. "That's how I know he really likes you. Flirting is like breathing to Clay. In you, he's finally found his perfect partner. You give it back to him as fast as he can shovel it. You keep him in his place."

Kelsey tilted her head. "It's a sacred duty."

Lila chuckled. "I guarantee he's working up his nerve to kiss you."

Kelsey gave a very unladylike snort. "Clay McKendry isn't exactly a shrinking violet. If he wanted to kiss me, he would have."

"He's making up his mind whether he's going to be brave or not."

Kelsey grunted. "It would not do for me to get my hands on that Angela person."

"Clay seems all fun and froth, but he's a serious guy. When he kisses you—"

"If he kisses me." Kelsey rolled her eyes.

"*When* he kisses you, he will mean it. For real and forever."

Kelsey let out a sigh. "In the meantime?"

"Pray for wisdom and patience." Lila slipped her arm around her. "Trust me, I know. For every one step forward, expect to take two steps back."

Kelsey gritted her teeth. "Greaaat…"

Later that afternoon, Clay brought Kelsey back to the Jar to meet up with his grandmother and Mr. Howard for the cake tasting. Owing to the festival, the diner had extended its hours just for today. Kara walked them to the corner booth where Maddie Lovett, one of Kara's scholarship recipients, had set up her wares.

Maddie was young, eager to please and extremely talented. They had a good time selecting options for Nana Dot's wedding cake. The buttercream secret family recipe was out of this world.

The apprentice baker had just packed up and left them to finish off the samples with their coffee when Kelsey's phone buzzed. She glanced at caller ID. A *V* creased the space between her brows. "It's Felicity from the resort."

Clay dabbed at the cake crumbs with his finger. "Working over a holiday weekend? That's what I call dedication."

"Excuse me." Kelsey slid out of the booth. "I should take this." She retreated to a quieter spot near an unoccupied stool at the counter. Hand over her ear, she spoke rapidly into the phone. Her features fell.

Concerned, he was about to go after her when Howard beckoned someone near the door.

"Son!" Howard slid out. "Over here. Boyd."

Clay whipped around.

His first impression of Kelsey's father was that she'd inherited her eyes and dark hair from him. The dash of silver at his temples gave him a distinguished air.

"Look, Polka Dot." Howard helped Nana ease out of the booth. "Boyd's paid us a surprise visit to meet you."

But given the man's startled expression, Clay wondered if Boyd Howard Summerfield III wasn't the one surprised. Stock-still at the entrance, his eyes panned furtively as if seeking an escape.

Nixing any plan to flee, however, Trudy took hold of his arm. "Howie's son. We've heard so much about you."

Clay wasn't surprised his aunt had latched onto him.

He could see how she would find the widower attractive. Women went gaga for the whole tall, dark and handsome if slightly brooding thing.

She tugged him over to the booth. Clay stood up.

Clearly delighted, Howard clapped his son on the back and made the introductions. "Why didn't you tell us you were coming?" Howard grinned.

"Are you able to stay in Truelove awhile?" Nana clasped his hand. "We would love for you to come out to the ranch and visit us a spell."

"How could you do this, Dad?" Kelsey growled.

Everyone turned.

Fists balled, she radiated sheer fury.

Clay took a step toward her. "What's wrong, Kelsey?"

"I'll tell you what's wrong." She jabbed her finger in the air between her and her father. "Suddenly the resort finds itself double-booked for December third."

Clay's stomach tanked. After all her hard work…

"Oh no." Howard slumped. "What happened, honey-bun?"

Nana rallied. "Doesn't matter. We'll find something else. Something better."

"There isn't anything else available, much less better." She clenched her teeth. "But you knew that didn't you, Dad? And you waited deliberately, all this time, until Thanksgiving weekend when you knew it would be impossible to rebook somewhere else, to sabotage Grampy's wedding."

Howard's brow wrinkled. "Son?"

Boyd Summerfield pursed his lips. "Surely this is not the place to discuss this little misunderstanding. The inn double-booked the date."

"And how would you know that, Dad, unless you were in this up to your eyeballs?" All five foot four of her,

Kelsey got in his space. "What did you promise Randleman to insure we lost the venue?"

"I'm sure I have no idea—"

"You used me." Kelsey quivered. "When you offered me a job at Summerfield after putting on this wedding, I believed you and I were finally connecting with each other."

Clay's gaze pinged between father and daughter. "What job offer?"

Howard's son blew out an exasperated breath. "What do you need a job for, Kelsey?" He threw out his hands. "Grampy and Granna made sure you'd be well provided for, job or no job. You've got your trust fund to rely upon."

Clay went rigid. "What trust fund?"

"You were only pumping for information to destroy Grampy's wedding. How could you, Dad?" she whispered. "How could you?"

Every doubt, every insecurity, the very worst part of himself rose inside Clay.

Howard and Boyd started to argue.

"Stop it!" Nana put her hands over her ears. "Stop it right now. This isn't what a family is supposed to be. I won't be the wedge that comes between a father and son."

Her breaths becoming increasingly short, she put out her hand to steady herself against the edge of the table.

Clay moved to her side. "Nana, what is it? What's wrong?"

She shook her head wildly. "I can't do this, Howard. I can't marry you. The wedding is off."

Howard gasped. "Dot, no. We can work this—"

"It's my heart." Chest heaving, she reached for her grandson. "Help me, Clay."

Then, her knees buckled, and she started a slow descent to the floor.

Chapter Thirteen

Catching his grandmother in his arms, Clay eased her into a chair. Her breathing was labored. She clutched her shoulder. Her eyes behind the lens of her glasses were wide with terror.

"Aunt Trudy!" he yelled. "Call 9-1-1."

Kelsey's father shrank back. Howard staggered. A roaring filled Clay's head. Someone must have summoned Dr. Jernigan. Gripping his medical bag, he rushed into the café.

"Clay." Kara tugged at his arm. "Give the doc room to take care of her."

Sick with fear, he allowed himself to be trundled aside. The diner had gone quiet. No one moved. It felt to him as if no one breathed. At the table beneath the community bulletin board, the matchmakers prayed for his grandmother.

He put a shaky hand to his head. This couldn't be happening. Why had this happened? His gaze landed on Boyd Summerfield.

Clay lunged. "You did this!" He jabbed his finger in the man's face, which had gone pale. "This is your fault."

The petite Kara grabbed hold of his shoulder. "This isn't the time. Nor the place."

Kelsey eased her trembling grandfather into a chair. She touched Clay's arm. "What can I do?"

"Haven't you done enough?" Scowling, he shook off her hand. "Nobody needs or wants you here."

She reeled as if he'd struck her.

As soon as the words left his mouth, he was sorry. If he lived to be a hundred, he'd never forget the look on her face. But she was a Summerfield and well-schooled by the people who inhabited her world.

Within seconds, she'd composed her features. Only her white knuckles where she clutched her purse betrayed any hint of inner turmoil. "I'll be at Martha Alice's. Please let me know how Miss Dot is doing."

Lips tight, he gave her a short, clipped nod. She left the café. Siren blaring, an ambulance arrived from the fire station across the square.

Dr. Jernigan finished checking Nana's vitals. Easing back, he reslung the stethoscope around his neck. "Frightening as it was, I believe this is a panic attack."

Trudy sagged against Clay. "Thank You, God."

"As a precaution, though, I'd prefer Dorothy go to County for a thorough assessment." Dr. Jernigan signaled Luke Morgan and another paramedic. The two men on either side helped Nana to her feet.

The panic attack must have frightened his grandmother. It had certainly terrified Clay and everyone else. She went onto the gurney without protest.

Boyd stepped forward. "Let me drive you, Dad."

Howard pushed him away. "Like you care."

Boyd's face fell.

Nana reached out her hand. "Howard?"

Kelsey's grandfather grasped hold. "I'm here, Polka Dot."

Her mouth wobbled. "I didn't mean what I said. I love you, Howard. Don't leave me."

"I love you, too." Standing by her side, Kelsey's grandfather kissed Nana's forehead. "Don't you worry. I'm not going anywhere." Straightening, he glared at his son, Clay and then Luke. "I'm going with Dot in the ambulance."

Luke nodded. "Yes, sir, Mr. Summerfield. Of course."

Clay followed them onto the sidewalk. "I'll drive you, Aunt Trudy."

"You head on, nephew."

Trudy locked eyes with Summerfield. If looks could have killed, Boyd would have been incinerated on the spot. "Since you're so eager to drive to County, you can take me and prove you're not the total jerk I'm thinking you are." She jabbed her finger into his suit coat.

He flinched.

"Along the way, you and I are going to have a little chat."

Kelsey's father dropped his gaze to the pavement.

His aunt's mouth thinned. "And by chat, I mean I'm going to talk and you're going to listen. Got it?"

Boyd swallowed. "Yes, ma'am."

Clay wasn't sure what to make of his usually happy-go-lucky aunt. He was only glad he wasn't on the receiving end of her wrath. McKendry women didn't get riled often, but when they did? Katie, bar the door.

At the hospital, Clay sat in the waiting room, reassuring an anxious Howard. While they awaited word on Nana, he combed through every conversation he'd ever had with Kelsey, searching for clues she'd been playing him.

He'd believed he'd been betrayed by the best when Angela threw him over for the bright lights of Raleigh and the more upwardly mobile podiatrist. But he never saw Kelsey's treachery coming.

Bottom line, he was a fool for trusting someone like her. For lowering his guard. For ever falling— He gritted his teeth.

He was not in love with her.

She wasn't the woman he'd believed her to be. She'd

lied. Hurt his grandmother. For the sake of winning her father's favor to get a job.

What kind of people had he and Nana Dot gotten involved with? These Summerfields had ice water running through their veins. And then there was the whole trust-fund thing.

Fear and insecurity raged inside him. What a chump he had been to have ever thought there might be a future with her. They were from two totally incompatible worlds.

Boyd and Trudy joined them in the waiting room. Based on Summerfield's shamefaced look, he suspected Trudy had had her say and then some. Fire still sparked in her eyes.

Kelsey's father touched Howard's arm. "I need to apologize. I had no right to interfere. There's no excuse for what I did, but I thought I was looking out for you."

Howard clamped his jaw. "You weren't looking out for me. You were looking out for yourself."

"I'm sorry." Boyd dropped his head. "I was afraid."

"Of what?" Howard grunted.

Boyd opened his hands. "Of losing you. I realize I've got control issues."

Trudy snorted. "Jerk issues, too."

Boyd flushed.

Howard made a noise in the back of his throat. "When will you learn that in trying to control everything, you only push people away?"

Dr. Redmayne came out through the double triage doors. After assuring them Dorothy had indeed suffered a panic attack and was being released soon, she allowed the family to see her in a curtained area off the ER.

Lying in the hospital bed, Nana Dot looked extremely fragile. Clay blinked away unwelcome tears. The panic attack had only underscored that the time he had left with his beloved grandmother was far less than the time they'd shared in the past. He wasn't ready, not by a long shot, to say goodbye to the feisty woman who'd taught him everything about life, faith and family.

Trudy rushed over. "Mama!"

Nana accepted her hug but then waved her away. "No need for the long faces. I'm as hardheaded as ever and fit enough to dance at my own wedding."

"Will there be a wedding, Mama?"

Nana Dot pleated the sheet between her gnarled fingers. "Unless Howard's changed his mind."

"My mind and heart remain firmly yours." Howard gave her a big smile. "Hello, Polka Dot." Stooping, he planted a kiss on her upturned face.

Boyd begged her forgiveness for what he'd done.

Nana looked at him a good, hard, long moment. "I'd never cut you off from your father, Boyd. That's not who I am or how I operate."

"No, ma'am." His voice choked. "I see that now. I'm sorry for misjudging you."

"Shall we start over, then? You and me?"

"I'd like that, Miss Dorothy."

She smiled.

Offering to drive her and Howard to the Bar None, Summerfield and Trudy went to collect his car from the parking deck.

"Clay, could we have a quick word?" Nana patted Howard's arm. "How about giving us a minute, dear?"

"I'll wait for you in reception." He shuffled out.

Clay swallowed past the lump in his throat. "You gave us a scare, Nana."

She held out her hand. "Sorry about that."

He took her hand. "Just don't do it again." He blinked

away the moisture in his eyes. "What was it you wanted to speak to me about? The ranch? Everything's fine."

Nana frowned. "I wanted to talk about you and Kelsey."

He pinched the bridge of his nose. "There is no me and Kelsey."

"I don't for one minute believe she was knowingly a part of what Boyd tried to pull, Clay."

He shrugged as if he didn't care one way or the other. "We're too different, Nana. Never would've worked. Better to have found it out now before hearts were engaged." He grimaced. "Poor choice of words. I meant before hearts got broken."

She peered at him. "I've seen how you are with her."

He clenched his fists. "I'm not in love with her."

Even as he said it, though, something inside him knew he was the one lying now. But he'd get over her. Like he had with Angela.

"I've seen how she looks at you, too," his grandmother said softly. "Clayton, my darling, don't let pride rob you of the chance for something extraordinary."

His chin wobbled.

"Talk to her. Give her the opportunity to explain." Nana squeezed his hand. "You owe her that."

He jutted his jaw. "McKendrys don't owe the Summerfields anything."

Nana sighed.

"But because you asked, I'll talk to her."

An orderly transferred Nana to a wheelchair. They found Howard in the reception room. Outside, Boyd pulled up in his SUV. Once Nana, Howard and Trudy were settled, Clay headed for his own vehicle. And the reckoning with Kelsey.

Driving to Truelove, doubts surfaced about the conclusions he'd jumped to regarding Kelsey. But mentally reviewing the reasons a relationship would never work between them, he stoked the flame of his anger. *Fool me once... Fool me twice...*

At Martha Alice's, he worked to get his emotions under a tight rein. He hadn't even gotten to the porch before Kelsey rushed out of the house. She must have been watching for him.

"How's Miss Dot?" She hurtled toward him. "What did the doctor say? Is she going to be all right?"

"A panic attack." He looked past her. "Just like Doc Jernigan said."

"I'm so relieved. Marth'Alice and I have been praying." She flung her arms around his middle.

He went rigid.

She lifted her head. "What's wrong?"

He kept his arms clamped to his side. If he so much as touched her, he'd lose his resolve. "In this weather, you should have a coat on. I won't keep you."

Slowly, she unwound from him. Her heels lowered to the frozen ground. "You were scared for Miss Dot. I get that. It's okay. I understand. That first day when Grampy hurt his—"

"Eighty years old, and she's managed to survive drought, storm, disease and widowhood without so much a flicker of concern." He glowered. "But let the Summerfields come into her life, and she has a panic attack."

Her eyes swam with unshed tears. "I love your family, Clay. I wouldn't—"

"I don't think it's a good idea for us to see each other outside of family obligations."

"You don't really think I sanctioned what my father did, do you? I would've stopped him if I'd known." She blinked rapidly. "You believe me, don't you, Clay?"

He didn't say anything.

"After everything we've shared?" She gave him a wobbly smile. "And then there's the whole Irish rock-band thingy."

"Maybe it wasn't about the job." He clenched his jaw. "But I think you'd do almost anything to win his approval."

She took hold of his arm, but he jerked out of her reach. "It isn't true. I promise you I would never—"

"Whether or not it's true is beside the point. Summerfields and McKendrys don't belong together."

"Your grandmother and my grandfather prove that isn't so."

Clay scowled. "That's different."

"How is it different?"

"Because you are the Summerfield, and I'm—" he clenched his jaw "—not."

Her eyes widened. "Is this about my trust fund? Clay, the money doesn't matter to me."

"It matters to me."

She lifted her chin. "Who's the snob now?"

He folded his arms. "Well done, by the way. When did you and your father hatch the plot? Before, during or after you had me chasing wedding venues over three counties? Got to hand it to you, babe." He sneered. "You Summerfields take the art of manipulation to a whole new level. Angela's got nothing on you."

Hurt flickered in her eyes.

"This would never have worked. A city girl like you. A country boy like me." His mouth flattened. "One day, you'll see I did us both a favor."

"Please don't do this," she whispered. "See me, Clay. Not the money. Choose me," she pleaded. "I-I love you, Cowboy."

Clay forced himself to look at her then. "But I don't love you."

Her breath hitching, she stumbled backward. "Oh." She wrapped her arms around herself.

Clay fought a visceral urge to take her into his arms. "We've said everything that needs saying. Goodbye, Kelsey."

He turned on his heel.

A quiet, devastating despair engulfed her.

Completely gutted, Kelsey watched—hoped—prayed— Clay would turn around, but his long stride carried him swiftly to his truck. He never looked back. Not once. He was done with her.

The red taillights of his pickup disappeared around the corner.

She let herself into Martha Alice's house. She found the older woman waiting for her, hands clasped under her chin. "You heard?"

"I didn't mean to eavesdrop, but—"

"We didn't exactly lower our voices. Just as well." Kelsey drooped. "The Truelove grapevine will undoubtedly do the rest for us on the off-chance people in the next county didn't catch it the first time."

"He didn't mean what he said." Martha Alice enfolded her into her arms. "He was upset by what happened with his grandmother. He wasn't thinking straight."

For a second, Kelsey closed her eyes, inhaling the faint aroma of roses that clung to Granna's best friend. "I think he meant every word." With a sigh, she pulled free of the older woman's embrace. "He appeared to have thought everything through quite well. Perhaps it's time I do the same."

She laid her hand on the newel post.

"Let's have a cup of tea."

She almost smiled. In the world of the two best friends— Martha Alice and Granna—tea could fix anything. Not everything, however.

"I'm going upstairs to pack." She climbed several steps

and paused. "I came to love it here, you know. Not only your wonderful house but Truelove, too. I'd actually come to see myself making Truelove my forever home. Surrounded by friends, family and faith."

Almost exactly what Clay once told her mattered most to him. She'd foolishly, as it turned out, believed she mattered to him.

"These last few weeks…" Her eyes misted. "I've had the best time of my life."

"Don't go, sweetie. Please." Martha Alice wrung her hands. "I know it seems hopeless right now, but things will get better. They always do. When he calms down—"

"It's time for me to go back h—" She swallowed, unable to call it home any longer. "To Asheville." She had to leave now before she lost her courage. "Thank you, Miss Marth'Alice. For everything."

The older woman's eyes filled with tears.

In her bedroom, she pulled out her suitcase and emptied the bureau drawers.

Home meant friends like Kara, Lila and Martha Alice. Home was Grampy, but thanks to her father's actions she'd never be welcome at the Bar None again.

Kelsey's mouth twisted. The Summerfields weren't a family. They were a corporation.

Home had come to mean Clay, but he despised her. That he could believe such lies about her robbed her of breath. She'd felt such a connection with him. Believed they understood each other so well. But for him to think her capable of sabotaging Grampy and Miss Dot's happiness? He didn't know her at all. Perhaps he wasn't the man she'd believed him to be.

Only thing she had left was her faith. Which made it sound like faith was a last-ditch effort. Not what she truly believed, she was just feeling sorry for herself.

She sank onto the bed. *Forgive me, God.*

It was Granna's faith that had made a home for seven-year-old Kelsey, who in losing her mother lost her father, too. It was Granna's faith that had given her the confidence to grow and flourish and dream. It was time to make Granna's faith her own.

When she came downstairs, Martha Alice waited for her. "What about the wedding?"

She set down the suitcase. "Supposing there will even be a wedding, they won't want me within a mile of it, much less a part of it."

"Don't be so quick to discount your grandfather or Dorothy."

But based on Grampy's reaction to the sweet potato rounds at Thanksgiving, she knew better than to expect the benefit of the doubt over something of this magnitude.

Martha Alice put her arm around Kelsey. "It would make you feel better if you'd allow yourself to cry. You never shed a tear at Joan's funeral. It's okay to cry when you're hurt."

She gently extricated herself from the old woman's hold. "No, it isn't."

At her mother's burial that long-ago day, her father had been angry at what he called her unseemly display of emotion. Summerfields must not, never should, did not cry in public. Even when her mother's coffin was being lowered into the ground. The next day, he had moved Kelsey into Granna's.

"What good would crying do?" Kelsey looked at her. "What good has it ever done?"

Martha Alice's face crumpled. "Kelsey."

She refused to give in to the tears that threatened to overwhelm her. Once she did, she wasn't sure she was going to be able to stop. Not for a long, long time. But the pressure inside her chest mounted. It was imperative to leave now before she lost it completely.

Kelsey gave Martha Alice a quick, fierce hug. Jerking open the door and gripping her suitcase, she barreled toward her car. Darkness was falling fast.

The café was closed. The end of the business day, the sidewalks had rolled up. Nothing much to do here at night except gaze at the stars. Not a bad deal if done with a particular cowboy.

No longer an option for her, of course. A sob forced its way out of her throat.

Cinching her hands in an iron grip around the steering wheel, she took a final look at the small mountain town that could have become her home. Where, for a time, she'd believed she'd finally found a place to belong. Her car rattled over the bridge. She blew past the sign.

Love had not awaited her in Truelove. Only pain and heartache.

Reaching the highway, she turned on the radio. Christmas carols rang out full blast. But it wasn't loud enough to drown out the noise in her head.

What was it about her that people found so hard to love? Her father. Clay. Why did no one but God and Granna ever choose her? She'd never been able to decide if she was just too much or maybe just not enough.

A lancing pain stabbed her chest.

In the privacy of her car, "Joy to the World" blaring, on a lonely mountain highway, she let the tears come. She hung onto the wheel as if for dear life.

Tortured sobs racked her. Stealing her breath. Gouging her heart. For what had been—the loss of Granna and her mother. For what never was—a relationship with her father. For what never would be—with Clay.

She cried all the way to Asheville.

Chapter Fourteen

Over the next two days, Kelsey ate a lot of ice cream out of the carton. In her pajamas.

She kept the curtains drawn. Lights off. With a tissue box handy in case she dissolved into a sudden storm of tears.

Kelsey didn't feel like talking to anyone, despite her phone practically blowing up with messages from concerned friends. All of them from Truelove.

Curling into a ball on the couch, she broke into sobs. Most of the people she loved best in the world lived in Truelove. Including Clay.

A man she'd believed would never let her down. But that's what people did. One way or the other, they always let her down.

Even Clay.

She scrolled through the texts and listened to the voice mails on her cell. It comforted her to know people cared. Martha Alice. Grampy. Trudy. Kara. Lila.

The outpouring of love and sympathy took the edge off the hurt. Not all, but some. She'd get around to thanking each and every one. Just not now. She just couldn't. Not yet.

Of course, the one person she most wanted to hear from

was the one person who hadn't reached out. Clay had made his feelings—as in, lack thereof—clear. But every time the phone rang or a text dinged, she looked at the caller ID, hoping against hope.

She'd learned from Andrew there'd been a confrontation between him and their father. Her brother and Nicola were leaving the company to start a new, nonprofit venture.

Reaching the umpteenth message left by her father, she stopped scrolling. She might never be ready to talk to him. Granna had taught her to be a forgiving person, even to those who'd hurt her most. Who deserved it the least. And she would. Eventually. She was working on it.

But she was tired of begging people to love her. She was sick of making excuses for their bad behavior. People either loved you or they didn't. And if they didn't, there was no way to make them.

Her future yawned empty and bleak. She was now without a job. Without a family. Without Clay. Tears flooded her eyes. She fanned her face.

Despite the blow she'd been dealt by people who should have loved her the most, one day she'd dust herself off and get back to living life again.

As a child, she'd watched her mother battle through unimaginable pain. Kelsey had the same fire in her veins. The same indomitable spirit. She was a survivor.

God had a plan for her. She didn't know what it was right now. But Granna had taught her to trust Him with the good and the bad. He alone was the perfect Father. The One who would never let her down.

Life would go on. Her gaze strayed toward the kitchen. As soon as she finished off another carton of Rocky Road.

The cell rang in her hand.

Shrieking, she dropped it onto the cushion. It wasn't a number she immediately recognized. Voice mail kicked in.

"This is Dorothy McKendry. Your grandfather has called you five times in the last two days. He's worried about you. I'm worried about you."

She pulled a blanket over her head.

"If you don't call me in exactly thirty seconds, I'm phoning the Asheville police to do a wellness check on you. One. Two. Three—" Dorothy hung up.

What?

She scrambled out from underneath the blanket. Inadvertently, her foot kicked the phone off the couch. She grabbed for it, missed and fell onto the floor between the sofa and the coffee table with a thud. The cell scudded underneath the sofa. Arm outstretched, she scrabbled for it. When her fingers finally closed around the phone, she clambered to her knees.

Leaning against the cushions, she frantically hit redial. The cell rang. Her chest heaved.

Dorothy caught it on the first ring. "Nice to hear from you, dear. I'm handing the phone to your grandfather. I'm going to the barn to give my idiot grandson what for the second time in as many days."

She didn't envy him being on the receiving end of Dorothy's ire. If she hadn't felt so low, she would have spared him more sympathy. But she was still working through the hurt.

"I'm sorry, Miss Dot, about what my father did to you and Grampy," she rasped.

"Dear girl, your grandfather and I know you had no part in that."

Her relief was such that she sagged against the sofa. "Thank you, Miss Dot, for believing me."

"We love you, Kelsey."

She blinked rapidly. The ever-present tears lay right beneath the surface.

"Please listen to what he has to say. We want you with us at the wedding. Here's Howard."

She was so thankful her father's schemes hadn't succeeded in robbing the elderly couple of their happiness.

"Hello, honeybun."

The sound of his beloved voice undid her. "Oh, Grampy," she sobbed. The crushing weight of sadness broke through her tight control like water overwhelming a makeshift dam. "I-I'm so...sss-sorry."

"None of this is your fault, Kelsey. Over the last few days, your father and I have had a series of painful heart-to-hearts at the Bar None."

The phone pressed to her ear, she climbed onto the sofa again. She was surprised her father was still in Truelove.

"What he did was arrogant, manipulative and wrong." Her grandfather's voice quieted. "But some of this is my fault. The result of how I raised him."

"Grampy—"

"As a parent, I failed Boyd. I put the company ahead of everything. Far too often, I left Joan to deal with him alone. I should've been there for her and for Boyd. When your mom died, he didn't have the skills to cope with his grief. He turned to the one thing I'd taught him by example would save him—work. Instead of showing him the all-sufficiency of a far better Father than I. A lesson I'm only now slowly learning, too."

His voice thick with emotion, she waited for him to regain a semblance of control over his feelings.

"You needed your dad, and what you got was two old people who loved you more than life itself. We rejoiced, despite the sorrow Boyd's neglect caused, that God had given us a second chance to do better by you than we had by him."

Tears trickled across her cheeks. "You and Granna more than made up for his absence."

"I hope you'll find it in your heart to forgive him, honeybun. The one person who could have helped him weather the storms of life was the one he lost. Although I didn't always appreciate it at the time, God has gifted me with the love, faith and strength of two incredible women. Joan and Dorothy. Not so alike on the outside. But on the inside—" his voice broke "—equally magnificent."

She took a quivery breath. "I-I'm happy you and Miss Dot are still together."

"The wedding is still on for next weekend, but we need our wedding-planner extraordinaire to make it happen."

"I love you and Miss Dot, but I'm not coming back to Truelove, Grampy."

"Summerfields don't leave a job undone." His voice warmed. "I know it's asking a lot, but we want you here to share our special day. Please, Kelsey."

Returning to Truelove meant there'd be no avoiding Clay. Yet after everything Grampy had done for her, she could no more refuse him than she could tell herself to stop breathing.

"Okay, but—"

"She said *yes*!" her grandfather hollered to someone in the background.

"Hold the tee shot, Grampy. I'll be there for the wedding, but until then I'm handling the wedding details long distance from Asheville."

"Whatever you think best. Gotta go, but we'll talk again later tonight to go over your new plan. Okay?"

New plan… Back to square one.

They said goodbye. Ready or not, it was time to dust herself off. Start planning a wedding and living life again. Even if it meant without a certain cowboy.

* * *

Alternate plans were hastily made. She checked with Reverend Bryant and booked the church for the wedding. Exactly what Dorothy had wanted in the first place.

Wedding-planner lesson number one—just do what the bride wants. She could have avoided a multitude of headaches if she'd only listened. She made arrangements for the florist to deliver the flowers to the church on Saturday morning.

Trudy took charge of calling the thirty-odd guests to inform them about the change in venue. With the exception of Kelsey's family, nearly everyone else on the guest list resided in Truelove. Rebecca's family and her parents would spend the weekend at the ranch.

Andrew's family had already decamped Asheville for a long overdue ski vacation at the condo this week. Day of, they'd make the thirty-minute drive to Truelove. Martha Alice informed Kelsey her father had become a fixture around the small mountain town, especially the Jar. She continued to dodge his calls.

With the wedding less than a week away, she was unable to locate another caterer or photographer. Thank goodness she'd booked Maddie Lovett to make the wedding cake. If all else failed, the guests could eat cake.

She checked the weather forecast with increasing regularity in the final days leading to the Big Day. Snow was predicted. Forget winter wonderland, though.

It wouldn't be the gently falling snowflakes she'd envisioned, but an honest-to-goodness, no-holds-barred, road-closing, electric-grid-disrupting, polar vortex of a snowstorm, swooping down from the Arctic.

The temperatures had already dropped. Winter had arrived with a vengeance. The weather person on television was calling it *the snowstorm of the century.*

She wore a path in the carpet around her living room. Due to daily marathon calls, trying to plan for every contingency, her neck had developed a semipermanent crick from propping the phone between her ear and shoulder. Somehow she'd managed to leave her earbuds at Martha Alice's.

Kelsey stopped in her tracks. What was she trying to prove? Who was she trying to impress?

No one. Not anymore. She only wanted the day to be everything Miss Dot and Grampy deserved. Time to surrender to the inevitable.

It was time to bring in the Double Name Club.

Swallowing her pride, she called GeorgeAnne Allen. Surprisingly gracious, the matchmaker suggested they meet for lunch at the Jar to make plans. Kelsey grimaced into the phone, but there was no point in postponing the unavoidable.

Kara met her at the door of diner with a hug. "I'd be honored if you'd allow me to cater the reception."

"Thank you." Kelsey slumped against her. "That's a weight off my mind."

"I'll do my best to replicate the menu you selected at the resort."

Kelsey shook her head. "Your cooking will far exceed anything the resort could offer. I trust you to put together whatever you believe Dorothy and guests would love the most."

The petite chef squeezed her hand. "I won't let you down." She motioned to the table underneath the community bulletin board. "Your wedding elves await."

ErmaJean Hicks waved. IdaLee smiled. Martha Alice beckoned her over.

Her eyes widened. The entire contingent of the Double Name Club had shown up to help, including some of the younger women who'd befriended her over the last month.

GeorgeAnne tapped a pen against a pad of paper. "Let's get started, shall we? We've got a wedding to organize."

Over the course of lunch, a flurry of plans were made. Everyone was eager to pitch in. Callie Jackson signed on to do the photography. Lila volunteered to oversee the decoration of the church. Trudy would wrangle the groomsmen into setting up tables and chairs in the fellowship hall for the reception.

Clay had told her once Truelove was the kind of town that would do anything for one of its own. For Dorothy's sake, the matchmakers had come to the rescue. Yet Kelsey couldn't help but bask in the reflected glow of their willingness to number her, if only temporarily, among their own.

The lunch meeting broke up.

Martha Alice pushed her chair under the table. "Are you sure I can't persuade you to have a proper catch-up at my house over tea?"

"Another time. I'm meeting Reverend Bryant at the church to scope everything out before I return to Asheville." Tea with Martha Alice would lead to probing questions regarding Kelsey's current emotional state. She wasn't ready to discuss her feelings for Clay with anyone, not even dear Martha Alice. Everyone went their separate ways.

GeorgeAnne headed toward the blonde, rather statuesque, veterinarian picking up an order. ErmaJean stopped to chat with the brunette pharmacy assistant, seated on one of the red vinyl stools at the counter. Which plus-one would Clay bring to the wedding?

Tears stinging her eyes—why had she not brought that dratted tissue box with her?—she thrust open the door to a mad jangle of bells and exited the diner.

She had a feeling the matchmakers wouldn't rest until

Clay tied the knot with someone. She hunched her shoulders against the chill. What did it matter, though? He'd made it clear it wouldn't be with her.

A snowflake landed on her nose. Startled, her gaze drifted to the leaden December sky. It was already beginning to snow? This wasn't good. Not good at all.

She drove to the white-steepled church on the outskirts of town.

After the wedding, she wouldn't be making many, if any, trips to Truelove. It wasn't just the cowboy she'd fallen for. She'd also fallen for the small-town charm and caring community in Truelove.

It was going to take a long, long time to get over Clay McKendry. Seeing him eventually get married and fill the farmhouse with little cowboys and cowgirls wouldn't help. She'd need to put distance between herself and the heartache.

Asheville was too full of reminders of that glorious day with him in the city. It no longer felt like home. Home would have been wherever her cowboy called home. Except, he would never be her cowboy.

Choking off a sob, she mangled the wheel.

She really wanted to pursue event planning. She'd enjoyed picking Felicity's brains at the resort. Perhaps the wedding coordinator might have a suggestion for getting started or refer her to contacts who'd hire her and provide on-the-job training. She'd take anything, anywhere.

Moving far, far away had never sounded so attractive.

At the church, she parked beside a lone sedan. Like something out of a Currier and Ives postcard, the church was extremely picturesque. A reception in the fellowship hall wasn't anything close to what she'd hoped, but with only a few days remaining before the wedding, she was thankful for a place where Dorothy and Grampy's family and friends could celebrate with them.

Waiting for her on the steps, Reverend Bryant ushered her into the sanctuary. She made notes on her phone. Dorothy's pastor was a kind, gentle man. She found him easy to talk to. If things had worked out differently, she could have seen herself making this little country church home.

She put away her cell. "Thank you for meeting me on such short notice."

He threw her a boyish grin that belied his fifty-odd years. "I'm looking forward to joining in holy matrimony those octogenarian newlyweds of yours."

She hitched her purse onto her shoulder. "We'll see you on Saturday, Pastor." Huddling in her coat, she returned to her car.

The wind had picked up.

On the drive to Asheville, more snowflakes floated out of the sky and dusted the windshield, but the snowstorm wasn't supposed to arrive until the day after the wedding. *Please, God.* There'd already been far too many hiccups.

Yet the unsettled feeling wouldn't leave her. By the time she reached her apartment, the snowy precipitation had increased. She bounded up the stairs. An isolated snow squall, she hoped. It would soon blow over.

Reaching the third floor, she ground to an immediate halt.

Her chest tightened. Her breath hitched. Anxiety and anger warred for prominence in her heart. "Why are you here, Dad?"

"When you didn't return my calls—"

"There was a reason I didn't return your calls." Her mouth flattened. "As you well know."

"Since you wouldn't talk to me on the phone, I decided it would be better for us to talk in person."

Brushing him aside, she inserted her key into the door. "You've wasted a trip." She stepped into the apartment. "I don't want to talk to you." She started to close the door.

His gloved hand caught the door. "Are you going to leave me standing out here in the cold?"

"Kind of like you left me high and dry on Granna's doorstep?" She wrenched the door from his grasp. "Yes, Dad. I am."

His eyes cut to the apartments on either side. "Must we have this conversation out here?"

She gave him a brittle smile. "Sorry to once again sully your sterling reputation. Summerfields prefer to let their dirty laundry molder behind closed doors."

"I'm doing it again." He sighed. "My entire life, I've cared far too much what other people thought. With the help of Reverend Bryant, it's a chain I'm working on freeing myself from."

Her dad was in counseling?

"I wasn't much of a father to you. For that, I will be forever sorry." His gaze locked onto hers. "It was my loss. I've missed so much of your life."

Taken aback, she let go of the door. It had never occurred to her he might come to apologize. Boyd Howard Summerfield III didn't do apologies.

"You might as well come in." She stalked into the living room, leaving him to follow or not. "I could've used a father then. Now we're more strangers than father and daughter."

He flinched. "I deserve that. But I'd do anything to rectify the situation between us." He followed her into the living room, but his trademark *I own the world* stride was gone.

She kept the couch between them. "Why the sudden regret?"

"For sabotaging the wedding, Trudy gave me a tongue-lashing I'll never forget."

Kelsey lifted her chin. "Good for Trudy."

He rubbed his jaw. "She also had a great deal to say about my lack of parental skills."

Kelsey turned away. Maybe she wasn't as good at hiding the hurt as she'd always supposed.

"I took a good, hard look at the man I've become." His face became bleak. "I didn't like what I saw. Nor the wrong choices I made after your mother died."

She wrapped her arms around herself. "I'm well aware how you feel about me. You blamed me for Mom's death."

"No, Kelsey. It was me I blamed. For failing her. I failed you, too."

"In a strange way, I always understood why you hated me, Dad."

He gasped. "I don't hate you, Kelsey. It's myself I've had a hard time loving."

She looked at him. "That would make two of us."

To her horror, tears rolled down his cheeks. "I'm sorry, Kelsey, for making you feel you weren't loved. For causing you to believe you weren't worth loving."

She'd never seen her father cry.

"Can you ever forgive me?" He took a deep breath. "Is it too late for us to be father and daughter? I know you don't need a father anymore—"

"No matter her age, a girl always needs her father, Dad."

"Would you…" his voice quavered "…would you give me another chance to be the father I should've been?"

Boyd Summerfield had never done anything but hurt and disappoint her.

Yet suddenly, anger and bitterness seemed such a heavy burden. Chains whose weight she was no longer willing to bear. If it were not for God's second chances, she shuddered to think where and who she might be.

"Forgiveness will be easier won than my trust, Dad."

Through the tears, his eyes shone. "Thank you."

Something clattered on the roof.

Kelsey darted to the window. "I hope that was an early visit from Santa and not what I'm afraid it is." She pulled aside the drape. Sleet littered the paved surfaces.

He checked the weather app on his phone. "It's not looking promising. The forecast has changed. The storm's arrived quicker than anticipated. Asheville is getting several inches of ice."

Kelsey's stomach twisted. A snowstorm was one thing. An ice storm quite another.

She raced toward her bedroom. "That settles it."

Her father ventured no farther than the door. "That settles what?"

"I can't run the risk of becoming stranded in Asheville." She pulled a suitcase out and threw in everything she'd need for the wedding. "Marth'Alice will let me stay with her. Hopefully, the storm will blow itself out before Saturday, but if not?"

Arms crossed, he leaned against the doorframe. "What is that clever brain of yours concocting now?"

Her father believed her clever?

She resumed her frantic packing. "I'm going to collect the flowers from the florist and take them with me to Truelove. Kara will let me store the buckets in her cooler at the diner."

"Will they be ready this soon?"

"If not, Marth'Alice and ErmaJean will help me finish them." She fluttered her hand. "Because that's the kind of town Truelove is."

He gave her a sheepish smile. "One of the perks of

Grampy marrying Dorothy, it seems the Summerfields have been welcomed into the Truelove fold by proxy."

She heaved a sigh. "I love that about Truelove."

"I love you, Kelsey."

Midmotion, she stopped and looked at him.

His mouth trembled. "I didn't say that enough to you."

Try never...

"But I do." An oft-concealed vulnerability crisscrossed his features. "Love you."

They gazed at each other across the expanse of the room and the gulf of years. Her heart pounded. Second chances came with their own sets of risks. She breathed a quick prayer for courage.

Catch me if I fall, God. Then she stepped out onto the emotional ledge with her father. "I love you, too."

He swallowed. "Could I hug you?"

She smiled. "I'd like that, Dad."

His arms went around her, and she closed her eyes. The familiar, warm, spicy notes of his signature cologne enveloped her nostrils. For a moment, she could imagine she was a child. That her mother was still alive. That she was home again. Resting his chin on her head, he wept softly. She hugged him.

After a time, he pulled away. "I don't want you driving to Truelove." He swiped at his eyes.

She opened her mouth to protest.

He held up his hand. "I'll drive you myself. My vehicle is better equipped to handle the treacherous conditions. Give the florist a call to let them know we're on our way. We'll load everything into my SUV."

Chapter Fifteen

Kelsey called Martha Alice, who promised she'd have a hot, hearty meal awaiting them. Granna's best friend also invited Kelsey's dad to stay in one of her guest bedrooms.

With her father's help at the florist's, they were on their way out of Asheville within the hour. They kept the radio tuned for weather updates. Already late afternoon, with the storm, darkness descended like a heavy curtain. Local forecasters were dubbing the snowstorm the Christmas Blizzard. News reports came of the city shutting down behind them. The roads were slick, but the ice changed to snow as soon as they left town.

Their progress slowed to a crawl. Just in time, they turned onto the Truelove exit. Word came the State Highway Patrol was closing the highway. Conditions continued to deteriorate. It had been hours since she talked with Martha Alice. The older woman would be anxious, but Kelsey had lost cell service not long after they crossed the county line.

The higher the vehicle climbed into the mountains, the worse the winds became, buffeting the SUV. Whiteout conditions prevailed. Somewhere on the right edge of the asphalt lay a massive gorge. One misjudged curve, one patch of black ice…the guardrail would never save them.

"I'm sorry, Dad." A hurricane of snow obscured everything but the pavement in front of the headlights. "I shouldn't have brought you out on this foolhardy journey."

They had to be close to Truelove, though. Surely this was the last peak before the road descended into town. In the green glow cast by the instrument panel, her father's face was grim but determined.

"As if I'd let you go out by yourself on a night like this." He flicked her a glance. "You would've come with or without me." He threw her a self-deprecating smile. "For better or worse, you're like your old man. Once you get an idea in your head—"

The car lurched and slid on the pavement.

Stifling a cry, Kelsey held onto the armrests. *Please, God.* The vehicle careened.

His knuckles white, he grappled with the steering wheel. His lips moved. Was he praying? Was it possible her father had truly changed?

The tires found traction. He regained control of the car. She gave his arm a squeeze. He turned his head briefly. In his eyes, there was gratitude and love for her.

Her breath caught. Hope swelled in her heart that a future might be possible with her dad. A way forward from the pain of the past.

Descending the mountain into Truelove was worse than ascending. It was nearly seven o'clock by the time the comforting twinkle of Truelove's downtown Christmas lights came into view. She felt weak with relief. The one-hour drive between Asheville and the tiny mountain town had taken three. She was thankful her father hadn't allowed her to drive the distance alone. She would've never made it without him.

He steered the car along Main past the shuttered café. "What should we do about the flowers?"

"The flowers will do fine in Marth'Alice's unheated garage until we can haul them to the diner."

Sheltered in the valley of Truelove, the wind no longer roared. Snow fell fast and thick, but he easily made the turn into Martha Alice's neighborhood. At least Truelove hadn't lost electricity. Which boded well for the upcoming wedding. Surely the storm would be over by then.

Martha Alice had the porch lights on. The white candles in the windows cast a welcome glow, pushing back the darkness. A phone pressed to her ear, the older woman peered out into the night. How long had Martha Alice been on the lookout for them? She must be so worried.

With a screech of metal, the garage door opened. Her dad veered into the empty bay beside Martha Alice's car. For a moment, he let the engine idle. Finally, he forced his hands to relinquish their death grip on the wheel.

Kelsey's throat clogged. "We made it."

"With God's help, we did." His gaze connected with hers. "And with God's help, I pray we will continue to do so."

She gave him a tremulous smile. "I think we just might."

Martha Alice flung open the connecting door to the house. Kelsey and her father got out of the car. Her legs felt as wobbly as a newborn calf's.

Which sounded like something a cowboy would say. *Clay McKendry, get out of my head.*

A pair of headlights swept across the open garage, and the door of a truck flew open. Outlined against the lights, a tall lean figure wearing a Stetson emerged. Clay stalked into the garage.

Bundled in his fleece-lined coat, he barreled toward her. A thunderous expression contorted his features. "Do you have a death wish, Summerfield?" He jabbed his gloved, index finger at her. "What city nitwit drives over the mountain in weather like this?"

"How did—"

"Martha Alice called and told me you were driving to Truelove." He waved his arms. "And that you should have arrived hours ago."

"I—"

"She was worried sick. I was wor—" He clenched his jaw. "I imagined you at the bottom of a gorge." A muscle pulsed in his cheek. "I was heading to the mountain to search for you when Martha Alice called again to say you were pulling into her driveway." Eyes blazing, he loomed over her. "How dare you put yourself in danger like that."

"Dad drove me here."

As if noticing for the first time they weren't alone, his gaze darted to her father, standing frozen beside Martha Alice.

Done with the emotional roller-coaster known as Clay McKendry, she drew herself up and got in his face. "What's it to you, anyway? Don't pretend you care."

The anger died in his eyes. "I…"

For a split second, she glimpsed something akin to anguish in his features. But without another word, he turned on his heel and stomped to his truck. Reversing out of the drive, he sped away.

She stared until the red glimmer of his taillights disappeared into the storm. He'd best heed his own advice. If he didn't calm down, he'd be the one driving off a cliff.

"When I called to let him know you were safe, I had no idea he'd react this way."

She cut her eyes at Martha Alice.

Knotting her hands, the older woman dropped her gaze.

Oh, she reckoned Martha Alice understood exactly how Clay would react. Probably bargained on it. Although, what it proved she hadn't the slightest idea. Except underscoring that he was a stubborn, pigheaded idiot. Which made her even more of an idiot for loving him.

Hands stuffed in the pockets of his overcoat, her father cleared his throat. "I didn't realize about you and Clay."

A sudden weariness assailed her. "There is no Clay and me, Dad."

He stabbed his hand through his salt-and-pepper hair. "I'll tell him you had no part in the stunt I pulled. I'll fix this, CeCe."

She almost smiled. She'd forgotten once upon a time before her mother's last, fatal illness he'd had that little nickname for her. "There's no fixing I'm a Summerfield and he is not." She squared her shoulders. "There's no getting around the insurmountable curveball of my trust fund."

Her father frowned. "He took issue with your trust fund?"

"Crazy, isn't it?" She moved past him toward the steps into the kitchen. "Created at my birth, a trust fund I've yet to gain access to and I've never actually seen a penny of. His pride is the immovable obstacle here, Dad."

Her father's eyes narrowed. "Immovable objects move when confronted by irresistible forces."

Kelsey's gaze cut to the driving snow outside the safety of the garage. "Miss Marth'Alice…"

"Don't worry." The older woman touched her arm. "I'll text Dorothy to make sure he got home okay."

"Thank you."

Drooping with fatigue, Kelsey forced down a few mouthfuls of the dinner Martha Alice reheated. But she soon excused herself to go to bed. Lingering at the kitchen table, her father glanced up from scrolling through his messages. "Good night, hon."

Maybe the day hadn't been a complete disaster after all.

She gave him a tired smile. "Good night, Dad. See you in the morning."

The next day, she awoke to a bright white, reflective glow spilling into her bedroom.

Pushing off the quilted bedspread, she padded over to the window. Moving the curtain aside, she surveyed the altered landscape. Snow had transformed Truelove into a winter wonderland.

A cold, brittle sunshine beamed from a blue sky. In the distance, she heard the sound of a snowplow. Martha Alice's street had been cleared. Dashing across the room, she tried the light switch. When the bedside table lamp sparked to life, she breathed a sigh of relief. So far, so good. As long as the streets were clear and the electricity didn't fail, the wedding could go ahead tomorrow.

The aroma of coffee wafting from the kitchen drove her downstairs. She needed a strong dose of caffeine before she tackled the remaining items on her to-do list. There were the flowers in the garage to be sorted. She needed to check in with Kara. She and Lila should start decorating the church.

She was still mentally reviewing the tasks yet to be accomplished when she ambled into the kitchen. Coffee cup on the table, her father was already at work, answering messages on his phone. He looked up. "Morning, hon."

Kelsey grabbed a mug and poured some coffee. "Hey, Dad."

"Um… There's something I'd like to discuss with you."

Her heart sank. That sounded vaguely ominous. "I'd love to talk, but I'm working against the clock today getting ready for the wedding."

"I understand. I'll be brief. I finally had a chance last night to look over your business proposal." He folded his arms across his chest. "You did a wonderful job explaining your vision regarding the company you want to establish with Kara MacKenzie. I crunched the numbers."

"Wait." She blinked at him. "You think me going into the event-venue business is a good idea?"

"It's a great idea." He nodded. "You identified a gap in the market, did your research and offered a viable solution to meet the need."

She sank into a chair opposite him. "You think my idea is doable?"

He cocked his head. "More important than doable, I believe it would be a profitable venture." He smiled. "I really think you're on to something here."

Boyd Summerfield was a shrewd, bottom-line, dollars-and-cents, profit-focused businessman. If he believed she and Kara could be successful, they would be.

She set the mug on the table before she spilled the contents.

He took her hand. "I believe in you, Kelsey. In planning Grampy's wedding, I've been impressed with how you've coped with one challenge after the other. I believe in your dreams, and I want to be a part in making them come true."

"Thank you, Dad." She swallowed. "This means the world to me."

He threw her a rueful smile. "It seems the entrepreneurial apple has not fallen far from the Summerfield tree."

"There's so much groundwork that needs to be laid in undertaking a new business. I'd want your input every step of the way. Especially in locating a site for the venue." She sat forward in the chair. "If you'd be interested, I'd love for you to mentor me."

"Of course, but I'm not sure you are fully grasping what I'm saying." He squeezed her hand. "I'm proposing a business partnership with you and Kara. I'd provide the initial financial investment. You and Kara would bring your particular areas of expertise into the operation."

Her jaw dropped. "You want to go into business with me?"

"With you and Kara." He let go of her hand and settled into the chair. "After the wedding, I'd like to meet with you both. We can talk through the particulars, and I'll have my attorney draw up the papers."

Jumping up, she threw her arms around him. "Thank you, Dad. Wait." Only then did something less pleasant occur to her. "You're not doing this out of guilt, are you?" She stepped back. "Or because you're trying to buy my affections?"

Somewhere in the house, a telephone rang. She heard Martha Alice answer it.

"I love you, Kelsey, and I look forward to us forging a stronger relationship." His forehead furrowed. "But when have you ever known me to let sentiment overrule good business sense? If it wasn't a good plan, I wouldn't sink personal capital into it." He looked mildly affronted. "Give me some credit. I'm a Summerfield."

Yes, he was. And so was she. She'd finally gotten a seat at the table. Thanks to her father's generosity, not only the seat but the table, too.

Clutching her cell phone, Martha Alice stumbled into the kitchen. "Sweetie?"

At the look in her eyes, the smile died on Kelsey's face. "What's wrong now?"

"Reverend Bryant called." Martha Alice bit her lip. "The pipes in the fellowship hall burst overnight. The entire space is flooded."

Staggering, Kelsey grabbed hold of her father's chair. For the love of Christmas weddings, would the mishaps never end?

"The good news is the sanctuary is untouched." Martha Alice placed a hand on her sleeve. "The wedding can proceed there as planned."

"But not the reception." She moaned. "What about the

food and Grampy's first dance with Dorothy? And the cake… And… And…" She sucked in a breath. "Maybe you should rethink going into business with me, Dad."

Getting to his feet, he put his arm around her. "This disaster is not of your making. If I hadn't booted you out of the resort, this wouldn't be an issue. You get them married tomorrow. I'll find a place to celebrate afterward." He kissed her forehead. "Don't worry, CeCe. This time I promise I won't let you down."

Last night when Martha Alice called to tell him Kelsey had gone missing while driving over the mountain, Clay's heart had nearly stopped. Grabbing his hat, coat and gloves, he'd plunged out of the farmhouse and into his truck. Pressing the accelerator, he drove as fast as he dared toward town and the road that led over the mountain to the highway.

The entire week without her had been excruciating. Driven by thoughts of her, he hadn't slept in days. He scraped his hand across the stubble on his face. Nor shaved. He'd barely eaten.

How had a little thing like her ever managed to get past his carefully tended defenses?

At the ranch, everywhere he turned he saw her. Wearing his hat. Scooping out the cow stall. Her attempts to lasso the fence post. He ached for her so bad he began to believe he might die from missing her.

Coming down the ridge in the driving snow, images of her replayed on a continuous loop in his mind. Ice cream in the city. Dancing the two-step in her apartment. Kelsey flinging herself against the stone walls of a Scottish castle and declaring she adored it.

He adored her. Not much use in denying it. He suspected he might even love her. There was so much to love about Kelsey Summerfield.

The truck flew past the icicle-laden Welcome to True-love sign. On the bridge, his tires skidded. Steering into the slide, he fought to regain control of the wheel. Going into the frigid, rushing waters of the river would help neither Kelsey nor himself.

It killed him to recall the accusations he'd hurled at her upon learning of her father's duplicity. Completely unfounded allegations.

Once he'd calmed down from his knee-jerk reaction, he realized she wasn't the kind of person who would have gone along with her father's attempt to ruin the wedding. That just wasn't who she was. Yet he'd allowed past issues with Angela to color his perception of the situation. It made him sick to his stomach to think how when she'd needed him the most, he'd turned his back on her.

Just like her father. She must hate him. He hated himself for hurting her.

A frightening image replaced his happier memories. A vision of her Subaru plowing through a guardrail. Of a sickening screech of metal. Of Kelsey trapped, plummeting to her death.

Of never getting to tell her how much she meant to him.

He started to shake so hard his teeth rattled. "Oh, God, please don't let me be too late. Show me where to find her."

Then Martha Alice called again. Furious with Kelsey—furious with himself—he'd quickly detoured toward the matchmaker's house. His ginger hair had gotten the better of him, and instead of embracing her, he'd lashed out at her.

Going toe-to-toe with him, she'd given as good as she got. But when she'd given him an opportunity to tell her how he felt, he'd drawn back as if from the edge of an abyss.

Clay McKendry was barely making ends meet at the Bar None. Kelsey Summerfield was a trust-fund baby. Beyond that, there was nothing else to say.

He'd fled the scene—and her stricken face—before he lost what little remained of his pride.

Clay returned to the ranch to find a tight-lipped Howard glowering at him and Nana Dot on the phone. *Thank You, God*, at least his parents were still at Rebecca's house until Friday.

"He's just arrived, Marth'Alice." His grandmother flicked him a stormy look before giving him a nice view of her shoulder. "Yes. Please do. I'll call you tomorrow."

Great. Now everybody was mad at him.

In no mood for another lecture, he stormed off to his room. Throwing his hat on the floor, he stomped on it with the heel of his boot. And flung himself onto the bed. That night, nightmares of what could have happened to Kelsey plagued him. Three times he awoke, thrashing in the sheets, drenched in sweat.

He was out the door for morning chores well ahead of dawn and Nana Dot. Despite the rumbling of his stomach, he decided to skip breakfast and avoid his grandmother.

Clay could hide in the barn all he wanted, but he didn't manage to outrun the long arm of Nana Dot. Although, this time in the form of his Aunt Trudy.

Midmorning, she stomped into the barn. "I've got a bone to pick with you, Clayton McKendry."

He kept his head down and the shovel in motion. "No time to shoot the breeze, Trudy."

Grabbing the shovel, she wrenched it out of his hands. "Hey!"

Clay scowled. Like all the McKendry women, she was tall and bony and stronger than she looked.

"I heard about your little temper tantrum last night at Marth'Alice's."

"From who?"

"Boyd."

Since when were she and Boyd Summerfield on speed dial?

"Stay out of it, Trudy," he growled.

His aunt tossed the shovel into a pile of hay. "I wish I could. But I refuse to stand by and watch my favorite nephew ruin his life."

"I'm your only nephew."

Hands on her hips, Aunt Trudy smiled. "Exactly."

"She could buy and sell the lot of us with the snap of her fingers. We'd never work." He shook his head. "Do you have any idea how much Kelsey Summerfield is worth?"

"Do you have any idea how much Kelsey Summerfield is truly worth, nephew?"

His heart pounded. Rubbing furiously at his eyes, he dislodged his hat. The Stetson fell onto the straw-laden floor between them.

"Looking worse for wear." She picked it up. "What happened to your hat?"

"Nothing," he mumbled. Except an encounter with his boot last night.

"I wasn't only commenting on the hat." She handed it to him. "Don't let your pride rob you of the best gift God's ever tried to give you, Clay."

He clamped the misshapen hat on his head. "It's complicated."

"Only because you're making it complicated."

For a long, long moment, she contemplated him. He squirmed under her scrutiny.

"I'm going to tell you something I've never said to another person, not even my mother, simply because it would cut her deeply." Trudy sighed. "She tried so hard to be everything for Gary and me when we were growing up."

"Trudy—"

She held up her hand. "Kelsey and I, bank accounts aside, have far more in common than you'd suppose. Both of us had emotionally unavailable fathers. We see ourselves forever and always through the prism of our fathers' neglect."

He swallowed.

"When girls like us don't receive the love we should have from our fathers, we struggle for the rest of our lives to believe anyone can ever truly love us."

His gut clenched. Was he any better than her father? His stupid pride had reinforced the already-negative self-image she had of herself. He fell against the stall.

Unlike his, Trudy's eyes remained dry. "Do you or do you not love her, Clay?" Her gaze never wavered.

"I do," he whispered. There was a sweet freedom in finally admitting it out loud. "But it's too late. I've ruined any chance I might have had with her."

Trudy cocked her head. "It's not like a McKendry to quit so easily. Now is the time to dig in your spurs and fight for what you want most. For the person you love the most. If it's not the ending you hoped for—"

"It's not the end."

His heart swelling with hope, he straightened off the wall.

She dusted off her hands. "I think my work is done here."

And his was just beginning.

They went into the house. He grabbed a quick shower and changed into his best jeans and boots. He'd just placed his Sunday Stetson on his head when his cell buzzed with an incoming call from a number he didn't recognize.

"Hello."

"I realize you have no reason to do me any favors…"

Going rigid, he glared at the phone in his hand. How dare Boyd Summerfield contact him? He was about to disconnect—

"There's been a situation, Clay. I've been on the phone all morning. For Kelsey's sake, I'm going to need your help."

Chapter Sixteen

It had been a near thing. But between Sam, the matchmakers and other Truelove friends, they'd pulled it off. Clay called dibs for the honor of watching Kelsey's face transform once she got a gander at what they'd managed to put together one day before a wedding the likes of which Truelove had never seen. A wedding no one would ever forget.

On the Big Day, he filed into the sanctuary with the other groomsmen. Reverend Bryant stood at the altar. Clay, Andrew, and Kelsey's father positioned themselves beside Mr. Howard at the front of the church. Boyd squeezed his father's shoulder. Mr. Howard flashed him a smile. Kelsey's father was doing everything he could to make amends.

Earlier today, he'd asked Clay for his forgiveness in sabotaging the wedding, and Clay had given it. Trust was entirely dependent on how Summerfield treated his daughter henceforth.

Not that Clay would likely have any firsthand knowledge of how Kelsey was doing now or in the future. But he and Andrew were becoming friends. According to Aunt Trudy, Boyd and Kelsey had forged a new bond. Yet if Clay got so much as a whiff her father was giving her anything less than the respect she deserved, Boyd Howard Summerfield III would have Clayton Joel McKendry the Only to deal with.

The processional began.

Clutching her bouquet of crimson-red and snow-white roses, Kelsey started down the aisle. His heart slammed against his ribs. Her hair had been wound into a fancy bun, revealing the smooth curve of her neck and shoulders. His hand tingled with the remembered feel of her hair sifted through his fingers. The floor-length gown with the delicate beaded sleeves brought out the blue in her cornflower-blue eyes. She was so beautiful she took his breath away.

Kelsey's eyes—those beautiful eyes—connected with his. His heart stopped. He forgot to breathe. In that moment, time itself fell away.

There was no one else. Nothing but the music and her walking toward him. His heart welled with emotion. But just as quickly, she tore her gaze from him. He felt it like a blow.

She held her head high, the bouquet in her arms. Smile never faltering, she moved to the spot in the lineup opposite him. Rebecca and Trudy joined her. But he only had eyes for the woman who'd lassoed a don't-fence-me-in cowboy like himself.

Oh, Keltz, his heart whispered. *Please. Give me another chance to show you how much I love you.*

In a matching tux, five-year-old Peter bounded down the aisle as a fast clip, ready to be out of the limelight. He stuttered to a stop at his designated place in front of his Uncle Clay.

"Whew!" The little boy blew out an exaggerated breath. "Glad that's over."

Subdued laughter tittered among the assembled guests.

"You did great, bud," he whispered.

His nephew waggled his fingers at his mom. Smiling, Kelsey's eyes found Clay's. He found himself oddly reassured. Perhaps she wasn't as angry with him as he feared. He drank in her loveliness.

Eloise danced down the aisle, like her aunt always a bundle of energy. She scattered the petals hither and yon before sliding into place at Kelsey's elbow. Eloise grinned at him. He winked.

A rosy blush bloomed in Kelsey's cheeks. Good to know she wasn't as immune to him as she'd like him to believe. The music changed. The congregation rose.

His father appeared with a radiant Nana Dot.

For Clay, the ceremony unfolded as if in a dream. Vows were said. Rings exchanged. He never took his eyes off Kelsey. *God, help me to show her how much I care. To tell her how much I love her.*

Chomping at the bit, he became slightly desperate for the ceremony to end. Reverend Bryant declared the elderly couple Mr. and Mrs. Howard Summerfield to loud cheers from the audience. The pastor instructed Mr. Howard to kiss his bride.

"Don't have to tell me twice."

With a twinkle in his eyes, Howard bent Nana Dot backward and planted a big one on her lips amid much hooting and applause. The music started again. The newlyweds sauntered down the aisle. Eloise and Peter followed the bridal couple. Peter's sneer expressed his opinion of having to touch a girl's arm.

"That'll change, little buddy," he muttered. Especially if it was the right girl. Once he'd found the right story.

Like the story of Clay McKendry and Kelsey Summerfield. Opposites on paper. Perfect in every way that mattered.

His saucy aunt gave the distinguished Boyd Howard

Summerfield III a sassy hip bump as they headed out. At first startled, Kelsey's father threw Trudy a boyish grin. Flabbergasting Clay and, from the surprise etched on Kelsey's face, his daughter as well. Leave it to Trudy. Boyd might not be as far gone from human emotion as he'd feared.

When it was their turn, he and Kelsey met in in front of the altar. Scarcely daring to breathe, he held out his arm. Her lashes flitted upward and down again as swift as a butterfly's wing.

But she took his arm. Together, they walked down the aisle. He laid his hand over hers, relishing the feel of her bare skin against his fingertips. Something sparked.

"So much static electricity today," she murmured for his ears only as they negotiated the length of the aisle.

His pulse quickened. "So much."

Once out of the church, she slipped out of his grasp to make sure the wedding party found their rides to the reception. She was the last to leave the church. He waited for her at the bottom of the brick steps. When she finally came out and closed the doors behind her, he straightened.

She'd donned the white faux-fur stole she'd chosen for the bridesmaids to wear in case of inclement weather. Snowflakes drifted lazily from the dark December sky. It didn't get much more inclement than a blizzard a few days ago. "Why aren't you at the reception?" She cut a look at the almost-empty parking lot.

"I was waiting for you."

"You didn't have to wait for me, Clay."

Okay… She wasn't going to let him off the hook that easily. Which was as it should be. He could work with that.

"How were you planning on getting to the reception, Kelsey, if I didn't drive you?"

"I guess I hadn't thought it through." She blew out a

breath. "Or maybe I was stalling. Putting off seeing the disaster that should've been Grampy and Miss Dot's wonderful night."

"It is going to be a wonderful evening." One foot on the step between them, he stuffed his hands in his trouser pockets. "Have a little faith."

She gave him a scorching look that could have melted snowdrifts.

He gulped. "I should never have doubted you. I know you would never have done anything to hurt your grandfather or Nana Dot. I'm sorry, Keltz. Forgive me. Please?"

She studied him for such a long moment he feared he'd lost her for good.

"Calling me Keltz won't always grant you a get-out-of-jail card, Cowboy."

She'd said *always*. Gratitude nearly buckled his knees. "Kelsey, I—"

"I need to supervise the reception." Moving past him, she headed for his truck. "We can meet for coffee next week."

He stared after her. Was she friend-zoning him? He settled the black, tuxedo-accessorizing Stetson firmly on his head. *Not so fast, little missy.*

They got into the truck. He veered out of the church parking lot.

"Wait." She turned in the seat. "Truelove is the other way."

He gripped the wheel. "We're not going into Truelove."

She frowned. "But the reception's at the Jar."

He drove up Laurel Mountain Road. "We're headed to the reception. It's just not being held at the Mason Jar." He steered between the two stone pillars.

Kelsey's eyes became huge. "The reception is at Birchfield?"

The rhododendrons lining the curving drive were alight

with a multitude of white twinkling fairy lights. Uplighting brought the birch trees into prominent display. He enjoyed watching the glow of wonder dawn upon her face. They crested the hill. Against the blue velvet of a mountain twilight, the house gleamed with lights, life and a party already in progress. She gasped with pleasure.

Clay bit back a smile. Nailed it. Job well done, if he did say so himself.

"How…" She flung out an arm. "Who did this?"

"It was a community effort. Martha Alice stole your sketchpad from your suitcase. Andrew cracked the password on your laptop. Lila kept you busy at the church. Your dad recruited me. Apparently, I'd listened more to your wedding ramblings than either of us imagined. I supervised the implementation of your designs." Parking beside her brother's car, he cocked his head. "What do you think?"

"I think…" she put her hand to her throat "…it's spectacular. Oh, Clay, it's everything I dreamed." Her eyes shone. "A real-life winter wonderland."

He helped her out of the truck. Golden oldies blared from within.

She clasped her hands under her chin. "But I don't understand how you were able to secure Birchfield for the reception."

Her father waited for them at the base of the sweeping stone steps.

"I don't have any details. I think that's a question best left for your dad to explain."

Boyd took her arm.

"Clay?"

Much as he longed to pour out his heart, now was not anywhere close to the moment he'd envisioned. He stuck his hands in his pockets. "We'll talk later."

Humming "Deck the Halls" under his breath, he went into the house to congratulate the happy couple.

"Dad? What's going on? How did we manage to rent Birchfield for Grampy's wedding reception?"

He smiled. "I didn't rent it. I bought it."

She sucked in a breath. "You what?"

"Actually, MacKenzie, Summerfield and Summerfield are buying the property. Mary Sue's letting us use the space on spec tonight." He lifted his chin. "I can be very persuasive when I put my mind to it."

She threw open her hands. "MacKenzie and Summerfield Squared could never afford a place like this."

"It's been on the market five years with nary a bite." He fingered his chin. "Did I mention Martha Alice is on the board of governors at Ashmont College? Talk about the art of negotiation. Granna's best friend talked them down a mil. We got the place for a song. We'll earn it back and then some, just like that." He snapped his fingers.

She gaped at him. "Dad…"

"Your grandfather and I are turning your trust fund over to you, effective immediately. Not that there'll be much left after renovations. Good bones, but the house will need updating."

A sudden terror seized her. "Suppose we fail?"

He put his arm around her. "The best investment I could ever make is making your dreams come true. And it won't fail. I know a good opportunity when I see it. Speaking of a good opportunity…" He glanced at the house.

She spotted Clay through the floor-length window.

Her father chuckled. "I think there's a young man who wants to talk to you. Badly."

"I'm still not sure how you roped Clay into this."

"Do you like what we did, Kelsey?"

She flung out her arms. "I love it."

"As for that immovable cowboy of yours…" he tapped his finger against the side of his nose "…never forget when we put our minds to something, Summerfields are an irresistible force."

The front door swung open. "Dad?" Andrew appeared, backlighted against the chandelier. "Sis?"

She caught her father's sleeve. "What about you and Andrew, Dad?"

"We're good. I've decided to invest in both my children's dreams." He patted her arm. "Try not to torture the cowboy any longer than absolutely necessary. He's a keeper, CeCe."

Racing down the steps, Eloise tugged them inside. After that, Kelsey was a veritable whirlwind of activity. And she loved it. Every minute of it. Almost as much as she loved a certain cowboy.

All through the sit-down buffet, she could feel his probing gaze upon her. No matter where she was or what she happened to be doing, his eyes followed her. But she had no time to talk. There was so much to oversee. The cake cutting. Toasts by the best man and maid of honor. Finally, the bride and groom's first dance.

"Polka Dot." Grampy smiled at his bride. "Shall we show 'em how it's done?"

Dorothy placed her hand on his arm. "Let's."

Unabashedly romantic, strains of "When I Fall in Love" filled the makeshift ballroom.

Across the crowded room, Kelsey locked eyes with Clay. A lump settled in her throat. Forever. That's what she wanted. Forever with him.

But what did he want? He'd denied loving her. Suppose he never did?

He said they needed to talk. What if he really just wanted

to let her down gently for the sake of their families? What if he'd decided there was no room in his heart for her?

Choking back a sob, her hand to her mouth, she rushed out of the ballroom.

Looking for a place to hide. Anywhere but here. Before she completely humiliated herself.

Again.

Brow constricting, as soon as Clay saw her features crumple, he made to go after her. But the song ended, and Nana Dot stepped in front of him. Kelsey disappeared into the crowd.

"I won't keep you, but I wanted you to be the first to hear that as soon as we return from our honeymoon—"

"Don't say *honeymoon* to me, Nana." He scanned the room, searching for a glimpse of Kelsey.

His grandmother rolled her eyes. "Once we return from our honeymoon, Howard and I have decided to move to a retirement community near Asheville."

That got his attention.

He frowned. "But the ranch…"

"I'm leaving it in your capable hands. We'll visit from time to time, but we want a place of our own where you won't cramp our style."

Clay made a face. *TMI, Nana Dot. TMI.*

"Howard is going to teach me to play golf. I'm going to teach him to enjoy life. Besides, I have a feeling you'll be needing the extra space sooner than later." She smiled. "Thank you for making this the happiest day of my life, Clayton." She gave him a small shove. "Go get your girl, honey."

Clay kissed her cheek. "Yes, ma'am."

Birchfield was enormous, but eventually he tracked down his favorite wedding planner.

He found her staring out at the night through a pair of French doors, which looked over a stone terrace.

"Kelsey?"

Her shoulder blades stiffened.

"Can we talk now?"

"I should see if Kara needs anything in the kitchen." She wrung her hands. "Make sure the getaway limousine has arrived." She made as if to move past him. "Or—"

"For the love of Christmas, Keltz."

He scooped her into his arms.

Flailing, she beat at his back. "What are you doing?"

Such a little thing. Light as a feather. Striding toward the French doors, he shifted her in his arms. Unbalanced, she squealed and clamped her arms around his neck, hanging on for dear life.

That was better. He grinned. Finding the handle, he threw open the doors and carried her outside. A scent of evergreen permeated the air.

"Put me down this instant, Clayton McKendry."

"Only if you promise not to run away again."

"I'm not—" She pursed her lips. "Fine. Let's get this over with, shall we?"

Without further ado, he set her on her feet. She wobbled.

He put out a hand to steady her. "One thing I should have told you at the church."

She looked at him.

"You are the most beautiful woman, inside and out, I've ever known."

Her posture relaxed a tad. "You don't clean up so bad yourself, Cowboy."

She shivered.

Clay took off his tuxedo coat and handed it to her. "Why is it in every big moment of your life you always lack proper outerwear?"

She pulled the jacket around her. "It's a gift." She raised her chin. "What do you want from me, Clay?"

He scrubbed his hand over his face. "I want to be in your life."

Kelsey's eyes narrowed. "What about City Girl versus Cowboy? Never the two shall meet, remember? Least of all, be friends."

"I don't want to be your friend."

She blinked. "Oh." She turned, but he caught hold of her arm.

"I told you I'm not good with words. I meant to say *just.*"

She bit her lip. "You don't want to be *just* friends?"

He ran his fingertip over her mouth. "Stop with the lip-biting. You're killing me."

She looked at him like he'd lost his mind. "Why does my lip kill you?"

He slid his arm around her waist. "Because it reminds me how much I want to kiss you."

"Since when?"

Clay pulled her closer. "Since forever."

Her eyebrow lifted. "So what's stopping you?"

Clay examined her features. "You?"

She smiled. "A dilemma easily solved." Rising onto her tiptoes, she tilted her head. He lowered his.

Her lips parted. "Kiss me, Cowboy." Only a whisper of a breath separated them.

Clay's heart seized. She brushed her lips against his mouth. Then pulling away a fraction, she winked.

"Absolutely killing me," he grunted.

One hand around the back of her neck, he pulled her mouth to his again. In no hurry, he took his time. Kissing her until he believed his heart might beat out of his chest. Until they were both breathless.

She twined her hands into his. "I thought you didn't want to be a *you two*."

"No one I'd rather be a *you two* with than you." He pressed his forehead against hers. "We go together, you and me. Like mistletoe and holly. Peanut butter and jelly."

"Just so you know, I actually prefer Nutella and jelly."

He sighed. "Of course you do."

"But I'm a Summerfield, and you're a McKendry. A kiss doesn't sweep those issues away."

"I said a lot of stupid things."

She smirked. "Nothing new there."

"I'm serious, Kelsey. I don't care about how much money you have. I just want you."

"And I don't care how little money you have, Clay." She cradled his face in her palms. "I just want you."

"We'll make Asheville and Truelove work. If I have to hire another operations manager and relocate, or travel the distance multiple times a week, I don't ever want to live a day without you in my life."

"Me either, Cowboy." She pressed her cheek against his pleated shirtfront. "I missed you, too. But you won't have to let go of your dreams for the Bar None."

He shook his head. "I won't let you sacrifice yours, either. You're in your element as an event coordinator, utilizing those oft-touted leadership skills."

"Glad you've finally come around to my way of thinking." She grinned. "But I won't be calling Asheville home much longer. I'm moving."

He tightened his arm around her. "You've taken a job somewhere?"

"I'm moving here to manage Birchfield, Truelove's newest entrepreneurial venture. And the trust fund won't be an issue much longer."

She gave him the thumbnail version of her partnership

with Kara and her dad. "He's loaned us the money to cover the sale price. Kara and I will repay the loan as the business turns a profit."

"Knowing your father, I'm guessing it was a loan plus interest."

"Exactly." She smiled. "Stick with me, and I'll make a business tycoon out of you yet."

"I intend to do just that." He wrapped his arms around her. "Stick to you. Though, I have to warn you, I can be a lot sometimes."

Her lips quirked. "I think I can manage."

Music floated out to the terrace.

She cocked her head, listening to the romantic ballad. "I love this song."

"What it says is true. I really couldn't help falling in love with you."

Taking her into his arms, they danced. "I love you, Kelsey Summerfield."

Her breath hitched. "I love you, Clay McKendry."

Snowflakes drifted from the darkened sky.

Kelsey was an extraordinary woman. And his life with her promised to be extraordinary, too. Lifting her hand, he kissed her fingers.

The music changed, becoming more up-tempo.

Grinning, he tangled her fingers through his. "How about we go show 'em, darlin', how it's done?"

Chapter Seventeen

Ten Months Later

"Where are you?"

"Hi, Dad." Kelsey pressed the phone to her ear. "I'm headed to the Mason Jar for a cinnamon latte."

"No time for that."

Okay...

Her relationship with her father had come a long way since Grampy's wedding. He'd taken to spending weekends at the ski-resort condo. They had dinner together at least once a week. He'd been a great support and mentor over the last year as she and Kara opened their new business venture.

"I've been talking to a guy who's interested in doing a prospective wedding with you. He wants to meet you at Birchfield."

"Sure." Coming into town, her car rattled over the bridge. "What day is he free to come by?"

"Today."

She'd gone to the Bar None to surprise Clay, but he hadn't been around. Maybe he'd gone to the agri-supply store. She'd drive around the town square and see if she spotted his truck. Driving along Main, her gaze flitted past the Allen's Hardware store, the bank and post office—Wait.

Was that her dad's luxury SUV parked outside the Jar? Not many of those around Truelove, where residents favored trucks. On Wednesdays, he was usually at his office in Asheville.

But over the last year, he and Clay's Aunt Trudy had been spending increasing amounts of time together. On the surface, the two couldn't have been a more unlikely pair, but Trudy made him laugh.

"What time today does he want to meet, Dad?"

"In fifteen minutes."

Whoa… Definitely no time for a coffee. But a prospective booking was a future moneymaker.

Her gaze scanned both sides of Main Street. No sign of Clay's truck. Giving the Jar and a cinnamon latte a last, longing glance, she bypassed the café. "I'm on my way there now."

Once out of the town limits, she veered onto the mountain road. At their peak this week, the trees were awash with color. The Blue Ridge glowed with the red, orange and yellow foliage of autumn.

Hard to believe it had almost been a year since Grampy and Miss Dot's wedding. The newlyweds had settled into life at the retirement community. Dorothy had taken up golf. On Sunday evenings, Kelsey, Clay and her father often went over to eat dinner with them. They glowed with happiness.

"So what's the story with this guy I'm meeting, Dad?"

Her car wound up the mountain.

"I've had a chance to talk with him extensively. He's a good guy. I'm praying this will work out for you."

She steered around a curve. It still took her aback to hear her dad refer to matters of faith. He'd made so many changes to his life. For the first time, she felt she really had a father. And she was grateful. So grateful for their improved relationship. Something she'd never dreamed possible.

Brown leaves littered the pavement, swirling under the tires of her car. "You think he could potentially prove to be an important account? For other events in the future?"

"Sky's the limit." Her father chuckled. "This could be a real game changer."

That sounded promising. Exactly what the fledgling event venue and catering establishment needed. She sneaked a glance in the mirror.

If she'd had more of a heads-up, she would have taken greater pains with her attire to present a more business-like image. Truelove had mellowed her. The client would have to take her—jeans, ankle boots and red buffalo-check shirt—just as she was.

"What's the man's name? Any details I should—"

"Um…" In the background, she heard voices and what sounded like rattling crockery. "Got to go."

"But, Dad—"

"Just one more thing."

She approached the stone pillars, marking the entrance to the property. "What's that?" She steered up the winding drive, lined with rhododendrons and birch. The morning mist highly atmospheric, the stone mansion loomed around the bend.

"You deserve all the happiness in the world." He cleared his throat. "I love you, CeCe."

She blinked at the still-unaccustomed endearment from her usually brusque father. "I love you, too. Is everything all—?"

"We'll talk more later. Bye, now." He hung up.

Okay… That had been odd.

She pulled to a stop in front of the mansion. She'd beat the client here. Great.

At the bottom of the stone steps, she took a moment to appreciate what she and Kara had accomplished. She loved this house even more than she had the first time she saw it. Kara had overseen the installation of a state-of-the-art commercial kitchen and also updated the expansive dining room. Kelsey had undertaken the refurbishment of the upstairs suites. They hired landscape architects to restore the overgrown gardens.

By spring, the venue had welcomed its first guests—a small, intimate family wedding party from Maryland.

Since then, Birchfield had hosted bridal and baby showers, girls' weekends and family reunions. Thanks to her father's influence, they'd hosted several Asheville corporate events. Birchfield was booked solid for parties during the busy, upcoming holiday season. Word had spread, and they were preparing for Thanksgiving nuptials involving a Michigan couple.

Kelsey loved what she did. In helping others celebrate the best moment of their lives, she'd found her passion. She rested her hand on the brickwork of the house. She loved bringing this house to life.

She could have never imagined a big-city girl like herself would be so content in tiny little Truelove. But it wasn't just Birchfield she had to thank for that. She and Clay had grown closer than she could ever have dared dream.

Her fondness for pickup trucks and cowboys had increased immeasurably.

When not working, they spent most of their time together. Which made it weird she couldn't locate him this morning.

Kelsey peered down the driveway. The guest was still a no-show. She hoped she hadn't come up the mountain for nothing. Might as well finish some paperwork while she waited. It was then she heard it.

She cocked her head, listening. Was that—no, it couldn't be. Bagpipes?

Out of the mist, a bearded older man appeared. Blowing into the mouthpiece, he played a rousing rendition of "Scotland the Brave." Behind him, another man stepped out of the trees. Her eyes widened. Was that Clay?

The piper led the procession toward where she stood, frozen on the steps. Arms at his side, Clay marched solemnly behind him.

In full Highland dress.

She gasped. Her cowboy wore a blue-green tartan kilt. An Argyll jacket with a matching formal bow tie. Sporran. And traditional Scottish brogues.

Reaching the base of the steps, the piper did a snappy about-face, returning in the direction from which he'd appeared. Clay stopped in front of her. The droning of the bagpipes continued long after the piper had been enveloped once again by the mist. The droning sounds echoed against the mountains.

"Clay, what's going on?" She propped her hands on her hips. "My dad said he wanted me to meet with a guy—"

"That guy would be me." He broadened his chest. "A guy interested in doing a prospective wedding with you."

She swallowed. "With me?"

"Definitely with you. Your father and I have spent a great deal of time talking this week. He, Aunt Trudy and the rest of the matchmaker gang are waiting at the Jar for a full report on how the next few minutes play out." His gaze dropped to the ground. "On how I pray the next few minutes play out."

The next few minutes... Was this what she thought—hoped—it was?

"Just so we're clear, why exactly are you wearing a kilt?"

"Last year, you wanted me to wear a kilt for the whole medieval-Scottish-wedding theme you had in mind, but I refused." He looked at her. "I've changed my mind. About a lot of things, since getting to know you better. Since falling in love with you."

He went down on one knee and opened a small jewelry box. Inside the black velvet lining, the Art Deco sapphire and diamond ring—from the jewelry store that long-ago November day—gleamed.

She covered her mouth with her hand. "Oh, Clay."

"Kelsey Summerfield, I love you." He threw her the lopsided smile that made her insides quiver. "Though it wasn't love at first sight, I soon tumbled fast and hard."

Tears pricked her eyelids. "I love you, too."

He tilted his head. "You're not going to cry on me, are you? If you cry, I'll never get through this, and I've got important things I want to say to you."

"I won't cry." She fanned her face with her hand. "I'm not crying."

"That's better." He nodded. "I didn't realize it at the time, but I think I fell in love with you when I saw your gentleness with Nana Dot at the bridal boutique in Asheville. And seeing you in your bridesmaid dress that day..." For a second, he fell silent as if struggling to rein in his emotions. "I've cherished these months with you in Truelove."

She put her hand to her throat.

"Darlin', you are the song I've always wanted to sing. The dream I'd didn't dare dream. The gift I never deserved—"

"The home I always longed for," she whispered.

His Adam's apple bobbed in his throat. "You are the perfect combination of sassy and sweet."

She smiled through her tears.

"You are funny and smart, and you could do way better than a poor ol' cowboy like me."

She shook her head. "You're the best."

He held out the ring. "Would you do me the honor of becoming my bride, Mrs. Clay McKendry?"

"Don't you mean, Mrs. Clayton McKendry?"

His lips twitched. "Don't push it, Keltz." He shifted. "Please say you'll marry me." He grimaced. "'Cause in this kilt, the gravel on my bare knee is killing me."

"I will. I accept. I do." She bounded down the steps. "I love you, Clay." She held out her hand. He put the ring on her finger.

Standing with a slight groan, he kissed the back of her hand. They shared a long look. Bright and full of hope for all the happily-ever-after possibilities tomorrow would bring.

Rising on tiptoe, she draped her arms around his neck. "You look mighty fine—just as I knew you would—in that kilt."

He laughed.

She cupped his cheek. "But don't go losing the Stetson just yet."

Giving her a cheeky grin, he wrapped his arms around her. "You like cowboys, do you?"

She smiled at him. "Who doesn't love a cowboy?"

* * * * *

Dear Reader,

Fatherless is defined as the lack of an emotional bond between a father and daughter through either death, divorce, abuse, addiction, incarceration or abandonment. It is estimated that one girl in four will grow up fatherless. Perhaps this was you. It was me. For many fatherless daughters, like Kelsey, their primary fear is abandonment, and their main coping mechanism is isolation. Yet despite the pain of their childhood, there is hope. These negative experiences often can result in many positive qualities in their adult life such as leadership abilities, empathy for others, resilience, strength and survivor skills.

Five things every girl needs to hear her father say:

- "I love you."
- "You are beautiful."
- "You have value."
- "I'm always here for you."
- "You can tell me anything."

Perhaps you didn't hear these things from your father. I did not from mine. But never forget what your Heavenly Father says:

- *... I have loved thee with an everlasting love...* Jeremiah 31:3
- *... I am fearfully and wonderfully made: marvellous are thy works...* Psalm 139:14
- *For I know the thoughts that I think toward you, saith the Lord, thoughts of peace, and not of evil, to give you an expected end.* Jeremiah 29:11
- *... I will never leave thee, nor forsake thee.* Hebrews 13:5.

Thank you for sharing Clay and Kelsey's story with me. It is through Christ we find our forever Home—the true Happily-Ever-After for which we were created. This is why I wrote this story. It is my prayer that you will walk in this truth about who you are in Christ Jesus. You are loved. You are beautiful. You have so much value that Christ died for you. He will always be there for you. You can tell Him anything.

I love hearing from readers so please contact me at lisa@lisacarterauthor.com or visit lisacarterauthor.com, where you can also subscribe to my newsletter.

In His Love,
Lisa Carter

COMING NEXT MONTH FROM
Love Inspired

THE AMISH MIDWIFE'S BARGAIN
by Patrice Lewis
After a tragic loss, midwife Miriam Kemp returns to her Amish roots and vows to leave her nursing life behind—until she accidentally hits Aaron Lapp with her car. Determined to make amends, she offers to help the reclusive Amish bachelor with his farm. Working together could open the door to healing... *and* love.

THE AMISH CHRISTMAS PROMISE
by Amy Lillard
Samuel Byler made a promise to take care of his late twin's family. He returns to his Amish community to honor that oath and marry Mattie Byler—only she wants nothing to do with him. But as Samuel proves he's a changed man, can obligation turn to love this Christmas?

HER CHRISTMAS HEALING
K-9 Companions • by Mindy Obenhaus
Shaken after an attack, Jillian McKenna hopes that moving to Hope Crossing, Texas, will help her find peace...and create a home for her baby-to-be. But her next-door neighbor, veterinarian Gabriel Vaughn, and his gentlehearted support dog might be the Christmas surprise Jillian's not expecting...

A WEDDING DATE FOR CHRISTMAS
by Kate Keedwell
Going to a Christmas Eve wedding solo is the last thing high school rivals Elizabeth Brennan and Mark Hayes want—especially when it's their exes tying the knot. The solution? They could pretend to date. After all, they've got nothing to lose...except maybe their hearts.

A FAMILY FOR THE ORPHANS
by Heidi Main
Following the death of their friends, Trisha Campbell comes to Serenity, Texas, to help cowboy Walker McCaw with the struggling farm and three children left in Walker's care. Now they have only the summer to try to turn things around for everyone—or risk losing the farm *and* each other.

THE COWGIRL'S LAST RODEO
by Tabitha Bouldin
Callie Wade's rodeo dreams are suspended when her horse suddenly goes blind. Their only chance to compete again lies with Callie's ex—horse trainer Brody Jacobs—who still hasn't forgotten how she broke his heart. Can working together help them see their way to the winner's circle...and a second chance?

***

LOOK FOR THESE AND OTHER LOVE INSPIRED BOOKS WHEREVER BOOKS ARE SOLD, INCLUDING MOST BOOKSTORES, SUPERMARKETS, DISCOUNT STORES AND DRUGSTORES.

LICNM1023